DISTURBANCE

Jamie O'Neill

Weidenfeld and Nicolson
London

ISBN 0 297 79492 2

Photoset and printed and bound in Great Britain by
Redwood Burn Limited, Trowbridge, Wiltshire

To F.R.H.

When I was fourteen, my father started on at me
about nudity. Men don't need to hide themselves, he maintained. We've all got the same mechanics.
No need for locked doors. That's the trouble with this
house, too many locked doors.

He took to walking around naked upstairs. He stopped
locking the door when he took a bath. There's nothing to be
ashamed of, he said. But I got around that. I, of course,
bathed every morning. Every evening as well, come to
that. But my father only ever bathed on Saturday afternoons, the same time every week, with *Saturday Theatre* on
the radio. I just knew not to enter the bathroom at that time.

My father then took to leaving the door open. I didn't go
upstairs after that, not on Saturday afternoons. When my
father started calling for tea to be taken to him in his bath, I
decided enough was enough. I brought him his tea, then
explained that I was feeling all hot and itchy with the
weather, did he mind if I just splashed myself from the
basin?

Not at all, said my father. Carry on.

I stripped off, splashed some soapy water round my
groin, and lathered away, making cooing noises about the
lovely cold sensation. My father turned up the volume on
the radio. I started towelling myself with the small hand
towel, slowly and ever so thoroughly, with my bum stuck
almost point-blank in my father's face.

1

After five minutes of this, my father said, 'I think you're probably dry now.'

And I had no more lectures about nudity.

In the breakfast room, the psychology books were relegated to a higher shelf in the bookcase and the language books came down again. 'What would you like to do?' I said to my father over breakfast.

'*Vorrei parlare italiano*,' my father replied. 'Now let's try a more difficult question.'

We were back to normal.

Of all our house, with its seven bedrooms, two staircases, sitting-room, dining-room . . . all that, only the kitchen, the breakfast room and my own garret bedroom were remotely habitable. Paint cracked everywhere else, tiles drooped from ceilings, there were indiscreet piles of rubble on the carpets. It grieved me of course, the dust, the disorder. But I could only do so much.

When I confronted my father with yet another reminder of all this dilapidation, he looked at me searchingly for a moment, then said, 'Rubble? What rubble?'

I looked around me. As luck would have it, we were on the main staircase. And the main staircase seemed to have escaped pretty unscathed.

My father was losing interest. I had to think of something fast.

'The banisters!' I blurted out.

'Banisters,' he repeated. He was making his way down the stairs. 'I wonder now what's the Italian for banister?'

'But Dad,' I said, following him into the breakfast room, 'they're a liability. All you have to do is touch them and they wobble. If anybody put their weight on them –'

'*Banistro?*' said my father. 'Sounds unlikely.'

'I mean used them as a banister, like they're designed to be used –'

'It's the only way to learn.' He was leafing through a dictionary from the bookcase. 'To increase your vocabulary.'

'I mean,' I said, 'if somebody ever leaned on them, by mistake even –'

'Ah!' said my father. '*Ringhiera*. Noun feminine.'

'But I mean, Dad, it's a liability.'

'Liability?' He smiled at me, wisely. 'I know that one. *Responsabilità*.' He offered me the dictionary. 'You can check if you like.'

I took the dictionary, returned it to the bookcase, returned myself to my bedroom. I don't think my father saw the house and the state it was falling to. I don't think he wanted to see it. He wandered about, delicately skirting the latest fall of plaster, remembering the Italian for 'cornice'. It was as though we inhabited different homes.

My bedroom was my refuge. When I looked at my room, with my bed so neatly made, the sheets folded that special precise way nurses use, my pyjamas on the pillow arranged to a perfect symmetrical shape, I could believe, almost, sometimes, that my mother was still alive.

That day was a Sunday. I spent most of it at my table in my room, where I had my jigsaw puzzle. It wasn't a very big jigsaw, in size. Quite small really, considering it had fifty thousand pieces to it. Every piece was black. Just black. And the completed puzzle was a flat matt black surface, shaped to a square. Sometimes I thought it was the most beautiful object I could ever hope to own. It was finished a year ago. The day my mother died.

I had known all along that my mother was going to die. The crockery on the dresser in the kitchen had told me.

I'd come home from school one evening. My dinner was

prepared – bacon, jacket potatoes and cabbage – informing me, if the page-a-day calendar on the dresser didn't, that it was a Wednesday. My mother and I ate in silence. Not so my father.

'Rio de Janeiro,' he said, 'eighty-four. Nairobi, cloudy but still eighty-three. Tangier . . .'

My father used always go through this routine at dinner. From the evening paper he'd choose the three highest temperatures from yesterday's readings. Then he'd turn to us, with only the faintest speck of an accusation in his eye, and tell us, as if we didn't already know, the weather reported for Dublin.

This time he said, 'And poor old Dublin could only muster forty-three with D for drizzle.'

My mother took away our plates and cups. Idly I watched her through the door washing them at the kitchen sink – when there was only the three of us, we always dined in the breakfast room. She dried them, returned them to the dresser, returned herself to her sewing. But I was no longer following her movements.

My eyes were fixed, aghast, on the dresser.

The cup from which I'd drunk my tea, which my mother had washed and dried so convincingly ordinarily, was there blatant as a public sin for all the world to see: she'd returned it to the dresser with its chipped side showing.

'Second-hand Citroën,' my father read from the classifieds. 'Now there's a thing. It'd be nice to have a foreign car.'

I turned slowly to my mother. She was busy with her needle. She had her hair tied back in her ribbon, but, unusually, stray strands had fought free. They were tickling her cheek and chin. She pretended not to notice. But I could feel myself their prickly irritation. She had her celeste cardigan

4

on, buttoned to the throat against the chill. Her attitude was – I thought – *desperately* normal.

She must have caught the vehemence in my stare. She looked up and smiled. But her smile was weak, I could tell, resigned – as though aware of her enormity but unable to act.

I stood up jauntily, assuming a returning air of nonchalance, and quick as a swat at a fly, I flicked the cup round to its proper position. The chip was concealed. I went quickly to my room.

Sometimes, when I stared at my completed jigsaw puzzle, I would remember things like that, about my mother. I did that Sunday, in the refuge of my bedroom, when my father had his first, minor, heart attack.

The stroke itself, it transpired, wasn't serious. A flutter in the pulse, he'd hardly have noticed it. If he hadn't at the time been standing on the stairs, that is.

He reached for support, half-leaned on the banister and, as in some awful classical Nemesis, the handrail gave way, and my father fell crumpling to the ground.

His foot was in plaster for a month. I brought his language books up to his bedroom, but he was listless, uninterested in them. When he was up and walking again, the first place he visited was church. And it was Mass every morning and rosaries every night after that.

I was fourteen then, and my father in his late fifties. Of course he already was, always had been, a Catholic. I attended the local Presentation Brothers' school. We were a Catholic father and son. But this was a different story. My father intended us now not only to be Catholic, but to be religious with it.

I gritted my teeth, persevered. Morning Mass was irksome, but not impossible. The church was near to my school, so with my father driving there every morning, the journey time was cut to a third. In other words I didn't have to get up any earlier. It was the rosaries at night that annoyed me. Television was switched off at nine, we had a good half-hour of praying. After that it seemed – even to me – impolite to turn the telly back on. I went to bed, untired and unsatisfied.

Morning Mass was given by an odd, oldish priest, Father Mulcahy. He had a rough, gruff voice, chesty from too much smoking, I presumed. He was always in a hurry, as if he had far larger affairs to attend to. Watching him was like watching a man in a silent movie, everything jerky, speeded up. The congregation had great difficulty keeping pace. We'd still be on a response while he was way down the bottom of the page.

My father had a maddening propensity to choose the front pew, as if he wanted the best seats. We were never early, we were rarely on time. This meant we had to march all the way up the aisle with all the heads turning, muttering at us. Worst of all, with no one in front to give me the cue, I found I couldn't work out when, exactly, to stand up, sit down, kneel down, stand up. My father was no help. He was always on his knees in church, his face buried in his hands, and his hands burning redder and redder, as if already licked by the flames of hell.

It was embarrassing.

After Mass one morning, I said to my father, 'That priest sure is in a hurry.'

He looked at me puzzled. 'Hurry?' he said.

I could see immediately that he hadn't been paying any attention. 'He goes at it like a dog at its dinner. You can hardly get a response in edgeways.'

My father shook his head quickly, as if clearing it. His eyes narrowed as he made quick spurting calculations. 'Of course he's in a hurry,' he said. He jammed his car into gear. 'It's the twentieth century.'

He was dropping me off at school. We got into a traffic jam and he had to stop. An unmarked van pulled up alongside us. The man inside – he had a beard and black eyes – wound down his window. He beckoned to us.

'Don't!' I said to my father.

'Don't what?'

'Open the window!'

My father made a smirking movement with his face. He wound down his window.

'Ballsbridge,' called the man with the beard and the black eyes. 'Am I doing right?' He had a country accent.

'Back up,' said my father, jerking his thumb. 'You're going the wrong direction.'

'Thanks now,' said the man, and he swung his van into a dangerous U-turn.

'Don't you ever worry', I said when I'd recovered a shadow of my composure, 'that a man like that might pull a gun on you?'

He looked at me with concerned puzzlement.

'No,' he said. 'Quite frankly, I don't.'

'Don't stare at me,' I said. 'Keep your eyes on the road.'

He started brooding again. I wondered what it was that so occupied him the whole time – in church, while he drove, any time and anywhere. He had a lot to brood over, true. After all, it was he who had killed my mother.

I found it embarrassing. But I gritted my teeth, persevered. My father's fads never lasted too long. Soon, I knew, we'd settle back into the in-between mania of naming things in

Italian. There were signs indeed, after two weeks, that his religious craze was already flagging. One morning, he slept late. We missed the bulk of the Mass. I thought that might be the end of it, but unfortunately that evening my Uncle Frank came to visit.

'How's the raving Trotskyite?' he said to me privately.

Trotskyite? 'The mad monk, you mean,' I replied, grinning.

I liked my Uncle Frank. He had a swimming-pool in his garden in the shape of an N and a shower separate from the bath. When I visited them I stood in the shower, hours on end. My Aunt Agnes never complained. She was a Methodist, and cleanliness came next to godliness.

They had an argument that night, my father and his brother. I couldn't hear what about. Only snatches. But after an hour or so, my father came steaming out and told me it was time for the rosary. My uncle shrugged as he passed me, circling his finger around his temple, nodding back in my father's direction.

'Loco,' he said. 'Get me Grange Gorman.' He was referring to our local lunatic asylum. Though he was a full half-hour younger than my father, he could talk about him in this way because he was a businessman, a successful businessman, with a house on the hill in Killiney and a swimming-pool in the shape of an N.

'We'll make him see sense. And sure if he won't see sense, we'll have to certify him. Must think I'm made of money, the joker. Get me Grange Gorman,' he said again, and chuckled to himself all the way to his car.

After rosary, I went to my bedroom. I stared a long time at the jigsaw. Sometimes it was more grey than black, sometimes it was blacker than midnight. Tonight it was just ordinary.

In the back of my mind, I knew, I was fiddling with something close to a madness. I had a notion to tamper with the jigsaw. Just, say, a quarter of a quarter of a corner of it. The idea was outrageous. Disrupting all that beautiful symmetry. My fingers were tingling with the mere conception.

It was dangerous territory. I turned away sharply. The notion had been horrifying, and yet, at the same time, like a late horror film on television, it was fascinating, seductive even. It had all the attraction of a criminal deed, done in the dead of night, that could never ever be discovered.

I sat on my bed. To engage my errant thoughts I reached under the mattress to check the sheet-folds. They were reasonable enough. A nurse would be satisfied, if a matron perhaps wouldn't. I wiped my glasses. I decided the only thing for it was to venture down to the bathroom, splash cold water on my face. I didn't get to the bathroom, however.

On my way to the door, inching past the table with the fifty-thousand-piece matt black jigsaw laid out squarely in the middle, my hand dashed out and, before I even knew it, my fingers had tugged on the bottom right-hand corner.

A tiny segment came away. I worked feverishly. It was a close-run thing, but in the end, after seven anguished minutes, I had the jigsaw completed again.

I wiped my glasses and caught my breath. I had a feeling of vivacity. I was vital, potent. It was dangerous territory, all right. You never knew what might happen with savage outbursts like that.

I decided it was high time I went to bed. I cleaned my teeth in the bathroom. In the shadows on the landing outside I fancied I could see a new chunk of masonry dangling from the ceiling. 'Another year of this carry-on and I won't have to demolish it at all,' my uncle might have said to my father. 'It'll go like the rest of the street and fall down on its own.'

My uncle called around again the next evening. He had the same raging row with my father.

When he came out of the breakfast room, he caught me at my perch on the stairs landing. He beckoned to me secretively. I followed him out the front door, through the garden, to the street.

'Let's take a walk,' he said. 'Just you and me.'

I wasn't too sure about this. I didn't like our street. Our street made me nervous. It sort of depressed me. I never spent a moment longer in it than was absolutely necessary. It was full of low cottages without gardens. The front doors led straight on to the street. Sometimes they left the doors open. And then you'd have to see wallpaper and things, smell other people's cooking. I could do without snatches of these neighbours' lives. They were the sort of places tradesmen-like people lived in.

'A walk?' I said.

'Just you and me.'

He seemed to think it was a treat. I gritted my teeth. 'All right.'

We walked along. I noticed he had his hands in his pockets. I did the same.

'Your father,' he said.

He sounded depressed. 'Yes,' I agreed, equally depressed.

'I mean of course I love him and all that. He's my brother. My twin brother. We were always close. Very close. Well, twin brothers usually are. Close, I mean. Nothing remarkable about that. Come to think about it, maybe we weren't all that close. I mean, particularly. Maybe we were only close in the normal run of things. Nothing special.'

His talk was beginning to annoy me. He seemed to be contradicting himself left, right and centre.

'But that doesn't explain why he's suddenly turned into a – a –'

Now I was with him. 'Lunatic,' I said.

He gave me a baffled look, the kind my father was always throwing at me. 'No, no, no. I mean this sudden socialist nonsense.'

'Socialist?' This was a new one on me. Did it tie in with Trotskyite, I wondered, rehearsing in my mind my uncle's greeting of the evening before.

'All this carry-on. Homes not offices. What does he want me to do? Homes not offices, I ask you.'

I had no idea what he was talking about. 'Homes not offices,' I scoffed, copying his sardonic tone.

'I knew I could rely on you,' said my uncle. 'I mean, look at this street. Who in their right mind'd want to live here?'

I followed his gaze down the long line of red and green front doors. Half of the cottages were empty now. Their windows were either boarded up or smashed in, or they had grimy curtains drawn against the light. At the end of the row stood our house. Our house wasn't too enormous. It only had two storeys, three if you counted my bedroom in the garret. But it stood gigantic against the tradesmen-like cottages. There was smoke coming out of our chimney. The sight of it pleased me, reassured me somehow.

Further along, there were vistas of other things, waste-land and walls, a power station in the distance, houses. But my eyesight the way it was, I could discern little beyond the perimeter walls of the old perfume works, where the weak sun glinted on the jagged bottle glass set on top. Cheval-defrise, my mother had called it. The street ended abruptly at the bricked-up works entrance. There was an air of futility everywhere, like the street, bereft of anywhere to go, had lost all sense of purpose.

My uncle was still going on questioning the sanity of anyone who would actually choose to live here.

'Yes,' I agreed solemnly, 'it's only fit for tradesmen-like people.'

He stopped in his tracks. 'Tradesmen-like people, did you say?'

'Well, yes.'

'What d'you mean by that?'

I stumbled for words. How else was I to describe them? After all, it was the phrase my mother had used.

'These people,' he said with the air of an appreciative man on a pleasant country walk, 'there's no cause to turn your nose up at them. They're the salt of the earth, sure, these people.'

I didn't know quite how to tell him it wasn't their salinity that I questioned, merely their proximity to my home.

'My father, your grandfather, built these cottages. For the workers.'

'What workers?' I asked.

'The perfume factory beyond. Don't you know anything of the family business?'

I believed I did know. But somehow – it's difficult to explain – sometimes, what with one thing and another, I sort of neglected to remember these things.

'But that's all changed now. I'm all for looking after the workers. Of course I am. I'm a Labour man, myself. I'll see them all right. Naturally I will. But not here. Not in these shambles. Sure, they'd have me up for rack-renting, housing a miserable mongrel in this old street. No matter what your father says.'

I still had no clear idea what he was getting at. But I gathered my father was against him. And that, certainly, was a point in my uncle's favour.

'Yes,' I said, shrugging hopelessly, hoping to please him. But he didn't even notice. 'Well,' he continued on, 'he can say what he likes. I've bailed him out enough times now. I'm not made of money. I've played banker to his follies long enough. The deeds are mine. Call it underhand he may, but that's business. It's a prime site this.' He was climbing into his car.

'Homes not offices,' he said again, chuckling away sardonically. 'I'll be back soon.'

He drove off. He had parked his car by the bricked-up entrance to the perfume works at the end of our street. It meant I had to walk all the way back home on my own. A hundred yards of those ugly cottages.

I'd feared I wouldn't make it. And I was right. Mrs Houlihan stepped out of her front door. I was trapped into speaking with her.

'Poor lamb,' she said. 'How's your Da?'

Normally I would have told her to mind her own business, but I was shocked that my father's state of mind was common currency with these salt-of-the-earth people.

'He's all right,' I said experimentally.

''Tis a shocking waste,' she continued. 'All these lovely cottages. After all of us being laid off from the works, too. A bitter blow. And your own big house with it.'

I twisted the corners of my mouth up, uncertain where all this was leading. Mrs Houlihan had huge gold-coloured rings dangling from her ears, two in each, the sort you'd pull a bull by. She leaned against her cracked wooden door, with the fringes of her shawl catching and pulling on the splinters as she breathed. I didn't know her very well. My mother had rarely spoken to the neighbours – except to complain, of course.

I wavered between saying something rude and something complimentary.

She thwarted me. 'Still,' she said, 'your Da's a fine man. Your Da's a decent fella. Handsome with it. Your Da'll see us right.'

There was an unattractive linger to her look. Her eyes were sparkling and she was smiling. She seemed to have all the time in the world.

'And that was your uncle you were talking to. Your Uncle Frank. He's a businessman. A right oul' businessman. And he's wrestled the works from your Da, so he has. These poor cottages, too.'

'Wrested,' I said.

'Rested? Who's rested?'

'The verb is "to wrest". Not "to wrestle".'

'You want to rest, poor lamb, is it?'

I had the feeling that everybody these days, as soon as I opened my mouth to speak, took on an immediate expression of puzzlement. My father, my uncle. Now, it transpired, even these tradesmen-like people from the cottages in our street had caught the contagion.

I decided it was time to go. I began moving off, walking backwards.

'Hold on a sec,' she said. 'Tell me, how's the jigsaw?' Her look of puzzlement creased in a second to a smile that lingered mawkishly in the drizzle. I could work out no recognizable reason for her good nature.

'The jigsaw?' I repeated. Then I remembered. Of course, it was she who had given me the jigsaw in the first place, when my mother was dying. She'd said it would take my mind off things. She'd been wrong about that. The jigsaw had been the greatest torment of my life.

'The jigsaw's all right,' I said. I was sick of the street and anxious for home. 'I have to go now.'

'Okey-dokey,' said Mrs Houlihan. 'Tell him we're all praying for him. Tell him we're all up there with him.'

I thought about Mrs Houlihan while I checked on my jigsaw that night. Perhaps I was wrong when I called her a tradesman-like person. She looked more like a gypsy.

Because my uncle laughed at my father's religiosity, my father naturally redoubled his interest in the Church. One Saturday, after early Mass – unusually, it had been given by the parish priest, more orthodox in his tempo and ways – my father didn't take me home but instead led me off to the priests' house.

'What are we doing?' I asked.

'What?' he said, as if really it had been my idea.

The housekeeper opened the door.

'I wish to speak with the parish priest,' my father said.

'Father Mooney is busy now,' said the housekeeper, importantly. 'With parish affairs.'

My father was flustered momentarily by this. 'Busy?' he repeated. He had a concentrated look on his face, as though he was trying to remember the Italian for 'busy'. 'Is there someone else I can see, so?'

The housekeeper obviously didn't like the look of my father, because she said, 'No.' She was unfortunate in this, however, because from behind her another voice called out, 'If it's them bastards collecting, Mary, tell them there's no one home.'

'No, Father Mulcahy,' the housekeeper called back, 'it's someone after himself who's busy.'

'Who's after him?'

'Who are you?' said the housekeeper to my father. But

15

she didn't give him time to answer. 'It's some man with a boy with him,' she said.

'I'll be down so.'

There was a long heavy thud on the stairs inside. The housekeeper opened the door wider, and gave us a look which said, 'You're in for it now and don't blame me.'

It was the usual morning Mass priest, the one who always careened through his service. Except, this morning, he didn't look at all like a priest. If anything, he had the look of a tramp about him. His dog collar stuck out one side of his shirt at a difficult angle. It looked like someone had tugged him there in a brawl. His clothes were all creased, like he'd slept in them. His face too. 'Who are you?' he said. Then he belched. 'Hard night. Never mind that now. What d'you want ?'

My father looked at him and at me. He shuddered. 'My son wants to be an altar boy,' he said, and walked off, leaving me behind.

'N ilus,' said Father Mulcahy, tasting my name and finding it insipid. ''Tis not a saint's name. There's no Saint Nilus.'

I felt I had let him down. 'I'm sorry,' I said.

'Mind you, there was going to be.'

He eyed me lazily, one eye cocked large, the other narrowed to a mean wink. Then he returned to watching himself in the mirror. He had stripped off his black shirt. I found myself infatuated with the unattractive folds of white flab on his back which battled against his string vest as he bent and straightened. He continued.

'True enough, there was going to be a Saint Nilus. 'Twas all in progress. Wheels were in motion. The matter was in hand.'

We were in his bedroom. He was shaving. For the most part he was addressing himself in the mirror, throwing expert strokes here and there with his blade. When he turned to me, every now and then, his mouth twisted to distaste.

'They'd beatified him even. The Blessed Nilus, he was. They were only waiting on final confirmation from Rome. And then the legate arrived with all the documentation with him, signed and sealed. The Pope had said yes. All was general smiles and jubilation.'

He ran the water, cleaning his blade. Then he rubbed his chin. It wasn't satisfactory. He went back to the lather.

17

'For the final test, though, they had to dig up his remains.' He nodded. 'This they did. Have you ever seen a corpse, what's your name, Nilus, is it?'

I thought of my mother. I nodded my head.

'Not a dead man. Dead men're all right. Dead men is natural. Dead women too. I mean a skeleton.'

I mouthed 'No.'

He was watching me. His attitude changed suddenly. 'Why d'you wear them glasses?' he wanted to know.

'Glasses?' I said.

'D'you need them?'

'Of course I need them.'

'Can't you see without them?'

'Of course I can't.'

He took this information in. He seemed to think it reasonable enough. He returned to the mirror.

'The bones are blanched white on a skeleton.' He had returned to his gravelly, cindery voice. 'And if you lifted the lid of a coffin, you'd find them all in the correct place, like twigs on a tree in winter, expecting spring. Touch the bones though, and they'd collapse in a heap to the floor. They were about to touch the bones of the Blessed Nilus when the legate peering in, cried "Halt!" '

He had his blade held high in the air. His hand was shaking. He was glaring at himself in the mirror, murderously.

'And do you know for why? I'll tell you for why. For the corpse's head was leaned against his shoulder and his arm was up against his mouth and there was a chunk out of his bone where his teeth had bitten in.'

He paused, chewing this over. 'Like this,' he said, and he took a gnawing bite at his own arm near to the shoulder. When he let his arm go, I could see the white teeth marks turning red. It was like the love-bites the senior boys had at school.

'They had buried him in a coma, you understand and waking up in the dark, in his dread he had gnawed away through the soft white flesh of his arm, to sever the veins within. They couldn't canonize him then, for he had taken his own life. It was clear to everybody present that he had lost his faith in the end. In the dark and dread of his extremity.'

He had finished shaving now. He splashed water on his face. The water dripped down his nose, his chin, dampening the white hairs on his chest.

'And that's why there's no Saint Nilus.'

I had no idea what to say. I was trembling. He was putting his black shirt back on again. Stupidly, I found myself concerned with the button formation. There was an extra strip of material that covered them up. So *that's* why you can't see any buttons, I thought.

'Take them glasses off,' he said.

I took them off, gingerly. I kept them on my lap, fiddling.

'On the table. Get rid of them.'

I did as I was told. But I had to keep checking back over my shoulder.

'Frightened I'll steal them from you?'

'No.'

'Can you see me now?'

I peered. 'I can make out a shape.'

'What am I doing?'

'I can't tell.'

'Nothing?'

'Nothing.'

'I'll tell you what I'm doing. You want to be an altar boy,

do you? Well, I have a queue for altar boys. I only take the best, I do. I don't take the riff-raff. The riff-raff can do late Mass. I only take the best. You with me?'

I wondered should I explain that I'd be just as happy, if it was all the same with him, not to be an altar boy of any description. I didn't have time to formulate this, however.

'Sit still now, till I make a portrait of you. I have to have a portrait of you before I can decide. 'Tis a serious business, being an altar boy. I have to see if you look the part. Sit still now.'

He rustled around, getting paper, I supposed, and pen.

'Open your legs,' he said. 'That's better. Boys your age should be in short pants.'

He drew in silence for a while, then he said quite suddenly, 'What d'you get up to in your bedroom? All alone in your bedroom?'

I considered telling him about my jigsaw puzzle, but I had a feeling that wasn't what he was getting at. Jigsaw puzzles didn't seem at all weighty enough to warrant the hard coming of his breath and the new tone in his voice.

'There's a cupboard there behind me,' he said. 'For brooms.'

'Oh.'

'You might think, if you looked inside, there'd be room scarce enough for one person, one little boy on his own, even, in that cupboard. And nobody else. You'd be all alone inside there.'

I nodded my agreement. Broom cupboards, on the whole, were on the small side.

'Well then,' said Father Mulcahy, his voice sounding peculiarly strained, 'you'd be wrong. You could encase yourself in an Egyptian mummy's box, all skin tight, d'you understand me? You could be short of breath, so tight the fit, squeezed tight inside . . .'

20

He was getting carried away with this tightness bit. His breath came harder and quicker, and his pen was making furious strokes on the paper. It stopped suddenly. He sighed. He swallowed. He stood up.

'But you'd never be alone,' he said. 'Your guardian angel would always be with you. Your guardian angel sees everything. You're never alone.'

He was at the sink again, splashing water.

'Put on your glasses and get out of my sight.'

I was at the door, leaving. 'Was my portrait not good enough?'

'What?' He sounded and looked exhausted. He had finished the bulk of his toilet and grooming. The result was that he still had a pinkish face, like a man in a minor temper, or a drunkard. He had big shoulders, broad: the type that would train young Catholic lads at hurley on a freezing Saturday afternoon.

'My portrait,' I said.

'Come back to me next Wednesday at five. We'll see then.'

Needless to say, I had difficulty sleeping that night. I kept worrying I might fall into a coma in the night and wake up buried deep in the dark and dread of my extremity. Then it got worse. I worried my mother hadn't really died at all, but had fallen to a deep slumber. Even now, this night, more than a year after, she might be turning slightly in her sleep, moaning softly. She would wake up. She would wake up and her fingers would stretch out and they would touch against something unexpected, velvety, soft. It was too dark to see, she felt about blindly, touching at first, then crushing her fingers. But everywhere she touched there was only the soft, half-satin, half-velvet confinement. Or dirt.

Dirt had got in. She hated dirt. It would drive her frantic, sensing the dirt around her, near her mouth, maybe, trickling up her nose. And she couldn't move. And in her desperation, she turned her mouth to her arm, the beautiful soft skin of her arm, the milk skin she was so proud of, soft like a kitten's fur, she called it. And she forced her mouth to open, with her pearly perfect teeth, but, before she would bite, she creaked her gaze towards me, all pain and reproach, but her eyes weren't there, were eaten away, just sockets in her skull, and she said, 'Why, Nilus? Why did you finish the jigsaw? You knew, Nilus, you knew what would happen if you finished the jigsaw . . .'

I woke up, screaming, 'It wasn't me! It wasn't me! It wasn't me!'

I caught my breath. I turned my bedroom light on. I wiped my glasses, fixed them on my nose. Instinctively, I checked under the mattress to make sure the sheets had not been disturbed from their folds. Everything was all right. My room was my own.

It was a dream. I couldn't go back to sleep. I could play with my jigsaw. But I didn't like doing that. Not after midnight. There was nothing for it but to go downstairs to the kitchen, make myself a cup of tea.

I rearranged the drawstring on my pyjama bottoms, found my dressing-gown and slippers. I turned on every light on the way down. It would've annoyed my mother – 'the Christmas tree,' she used call the house. 'Have we shares in the Electricity Board?' – But I could do without the dark, tonight.

I put the kettle on. I sat down at the table, in front of the dresser. I didn't want to look at it, but it fought for my attention. I'd left the dresser, when my mother finally died, exactly as she had left it. All chipped, cracked, rubbly. I'd known then that nothing could preserve my world from the chaos of her departure. Everything would end. The dresser was her shrine now, as in life it had been the altar to the orderliness of our home.

The crockery had been the first to go. I mean, after that dreadful day when my mother replaced the cup on the dresser with the chipped side showing. The days and weeks that followed were an anguish to me. I would return from school and with a ghastly certainty I'd check on the dresser. And true enough the cup was there with its chipped side showing. No matter how many times I might turn it, always if I checked again – morning, evening, evening, morning – driven by a hideous fate, the chip had worked its way to the front. Worse, the phenomenon began to spread to the other cups, then to the saucers. Even the plates suffered, rolling around in their grooves till an inexorable chip was showing. I felt that the world itself was cracking . . .

'Nilus! There you are! I thought I heard someone.'

I jerked up. My father had found me, half-asleep at the kitchen table. He went straight past me, over to the range. I realized the kettle must've been boiling away for aeons.

'What're you doing up this time of night?'

I shook the torpor from my head. 'I couldn't sleep,' I said, fairly lamely.

He tut-tutted. 'I don't know, Nilus. Sometimes you worry me. You really do.'

He began making tea. I wondered were we going to have a talk. It was a long time since we'd had a talk. That's the name he gave them. 'Talks.' If I got in first, I could at least set the agendum.

'Dad,' I said, not exactly relaxing back into my chair, but

23

taking on the head-leaning-on-hand position of a tired but serious enquirer, 'there was some sort of survey done at school today.'

'Was there?' He was measuring tea from the caddy.

'About fathers' occupations.'

'Well.' It wasn't an encouragement. I could see the subject didn't engage him.

'It's just that I couldn't work out what to write down.'

He poured the water into the teapot.

'And when I asked,' I continued, 'they just laughed at me.'

'Who?'

'Just everyone.'

'You want tea?'

'All right.'

He fetched some sharding cups from the dresser.

'In the end I had to tick "unemployed". There was no alternative, really.'

He laughed, like they laughed at me at school.

I could see I was getting nowhere with this. 'Dad,' I said, still in my getting-to-the-bottom-of-all-this voice, 'Uncle Frank says you're a socialist.'

'Does he now?'

I was surprised; I had his attention. 'A raving socialist, he calls you.'

'Well, he should know.'

'What does that mean?'

'No wonder you're never tired at night, Nilus. You're wool-gathering the day through. You must fritter your whole time away slouching around in a daydream.'

I could see he was in a mood.

He plonked the cups on the table, sat down opposite me. 'I told you last night.' He looked at me, as if wondering was

I his son, or who was I. His stern face melted a bit. 'You're still no more than a child,' he said. 'Anyway. Your Uncle Frank left home, God knows how many years ago. But he left home because he was a raging whatever-it-is, communist-something. Your poor grandfather was heartbroken. The arguments they had. And I was left to run the business all myself. And the workers' cottages. I'm no businessman. Never pretended to be. No wonder it went down the drains.' He seemed to find this funny. 'Perfume factory,' he said. 'Drains.' He didn't laugh, just smiled, knowledgeably. 'The thing is, the road your uncle took leaving home must've been in the direction of Damascus, because he returned still raging but no longer a whatever-it-is. The exact opposite in fact. Now, do you know?'

I nodded my head. It would've been really asking for it, to enquire, 'The opposite of what?'

I was sick of the 'talk' now. I said, 'Will you be going to Mass tomorrow morning?'

'If you want me to.'

'If I want you to?'

'Nilus, I'm not doing this for my own benefit. You think I enjoy rising with the lark every morning?'

He was definitely in a mood. 'I'm going back to bed,' I said.

'And turn a few of those lights off. It's like a Christmas tree, this place.'

I hated him using my mother's sayings.

I climbed back between my sheets in my bed. They were still warm from my nightmare. I felt, everything felt, unaccountably heavy. Such was my gravity that it was a full three minutes before I remembered to check my sheet-folds. I lay back, my head sunk into the pillow.

I hoped my mother would understand. It was my father

who had killed her, not me. 'It was Dad,' I said. I didn't say this to my mother. I tried not to think about my mother. Especially at night-time. I just said it aloud. 'It was Dad. He just never understands anything.'

When I was younger, my father didn't give me 'talks'. Instead, he told me stories in the night. My night, I suppose, not his. He was only trying to get me to sleep, out of pleasure's way. But I used to love his stories. They were about things that happened a long time ago – *fadó fadó*, as he called it. And because they happened so long ago, they never changed. And he'd sit by my bed, half-squinting away from me, like a mage glimpsing a faraway country, and tell me in his sapidly warmest of voices about hedge priests and blind bards and Cathleen ní Houlihan who appeared to poets in their dreams.

You could live in his stories, unchanged and unchanging, nearly for ever.

'Nilus,' he said, when I asked him about it, 'you've gone way past that stage. You're a growing boy now. A lad. You're a young man, for God's sake. It's time you worried about different things. Do you never think of girls?'

His question made no sense. I went to a boys' school. I lived in a street of tradesmen-like cottages.

'Girls?' I said.

'They're the ones with the bosoms, for God's sake.'

He was *that* capable of vulgarity.

The reason he'd always told me his stories half-squinting away from me, was that he always had one eye cocked to my bedside clock. Nothing he did was ever done thoroughly, with conviction. His put-down of me was tendered in such a ridiculously cold voice. It was as if the stories could change because I grew older.

I didn't argue. I didn't say anything.

The next morning – I mean the morning after the 'talk' in the kitchen – typically perversely, my father didn't go to Mass. He was up early, though. He had a hammer in his hand when I found him, and a bunch of nails sticking out of his mouth.

'What are you doing now?' I asked.

'I'm fixing the banisters, of course. They're a liability.'

'But it's time for Mass.'

'If you want to go to Mass, go. You can't expect me always to be indulging your extravagances. I've got other things on my mind.'

'Like what?'

'Like fixing the banisters.'

I understood the religious craze was finally over. In its stead, we were in for a fury of DIY and spring-cleaning.

'But why now?' I said.

'I thought you were the one always going on about dirt and dust and rubble, as you call it.'

'But why now?' I insisted.

He muttered something. Something about opening the place up as a boarding-house.

My Uncle Frank came round. My father wouldn't even let him into the house.

'Boarding-house,' said my uncle, when I joined him on the front steps. 'Who the hell'd want to stay here?'

'He keeps on about making it a "going concern". I'm worried he's planning on inviting the cottagers in.'

My uncle laughed. 'As for "concern", this place is mine now. And as for "going", the only direction this shambles is going is to the dogs. The way it is now, anyway. But we'll soon have that sorted. Won't we, Nilus? We'll soon clear the dead wood. Isn't that so?'

'Sure,' I said.

'Look at this –'

'Shambles,' I said.

'Shambles,' he agreed. He aimed a loose kick at one of the steps. Some mortar crumbled away. 'An advancing riot of anarchists, sure, would begrudge it a brick. Boarding-house, I ask you. He's really flipped this time over.'

The next few weeks were a chaos of activity. My father scattered his efforts, like he always did, starting one thing, then turning to something else. It was worse than living in a building site.

My bedroom was impossible. I would sit down with a shiver in my pulse, and contemplate playing Disturbance. That was the name I'd coined for the game of tampering with the corners of my jigsaw. 'Game' is too slight a word. 'Play' too. I'd worry my way through the yeses and noes, the pros and the cons, of a tormented indecision. I would feel vital, I would feel potent; but what if I failed to find the order again? Or worse still, should one tiny piece slip away, disappear even through the floorboards – what then? I was dicing with symmetry.

Then, with my eyes squeezed tight shut, unwilling to witness the deed, with my driven hand actually reaching out to disturb one-sixteenth of a sixteenth of a corner of the black surface, then the thudding would resound once more through the floorboards. My father was hammering again at the banisters. My bedroom was impossible.

I began to spend more and more time at school. There was nothing to do at school – I mean after hours. But at least it was tidy. And quiet. I just wandered around the corridors, counting off the aeons.

One evening a teacher stopped me. He bumped into me, actually. When I'd picked up his pile of papers for him, he said, 'Er, it's – er . . .'

I knew he'd forgotten my name. Teachers rarely remembered my name. The pupils weren't much better, come to that. 'Moore,' I said.

'Oh yes, Moore.' He was about to continue on wherever he was going, but he hesitated, inspected me. 'Tell me, Moore,' he said, 'why is it you're always walking in the opposite direction?'

'Sir?'

'You are, aren't you? Always in the opposite direction.'

It seemed churlish to disagree with a teacher, so I said, 'Yes.' Then, 'Sir.'

'I mean I don't think I've ever noticed you but you're bumping into somebody. Unexpectedly. Round a corner.'

I had an awful feeling this teacher wanted to talk with me. I had an awful feeling I would have to talk with him. I lowered my head. My chin pressed into the knot of my school tie. I would disrupt it, but . . . 'Yes,' I said.

'You're a loner, Moore, aren't you.' I knew he was looking down at me. I knew he was about to smile. His voice was a friendly, we're-all-in-this-together voice. I hated it. 'You don't have many friends, do you? Well, Moore?'

I lifted my chin, stared at him blankly, the way I knew would infuriate adults in minor authority. 'Sir?'

It did the trick. He took the folders I'd picked up. 'You want to be careful, Moore,' he said. 'Some people might think you were a loner. Others might believe you were giving cheek. Besides, you've no business hanging around school this hour. What d'you think you're up to?'

Later on, at home, I remembered what he'd said. I looked at myself in the full-length mirror on the inside of my wardrobe door.

'I'm a loner,' I said.

I checked on my jigsaw, then wondered should I masturbate. Nothing seemed worth it somehow.

It was five-thirty. Time I went to see Father Mulcahy. I pulled up my fly, and closed my bedroom door after me.

By this time, Father Mulcahy must have had a drawer full of portraits of me. He never let me see them.

'Do you draw a lot?' I asked.

'Mind your own business,' he said.

Hanging on his wall, in cheap plastic frames, were some sketches he told me he'd done himself. They were of churches. I looked at them. They weren't particularly interesting. 'My father doesn't know I still come here,' I said, apropos of nothing.

'Well?'

'He doesn't even go to church any more.'

'Well?'

It was difficult to get Father Mulcahy's attention, but I felt I needed to talk. 'He says the church is all baloney.' Still no real reaction. 'Turns out religion was just a craze with him. Like the Italian. And the psychology.'

'Psychology, did you say?'

At last I'd got his notice. 'Yes. He had all the books.'

'Psychology's an evil instrument of the Devil, sent to tempt us.' He considered this. 'Like apples in an orchard.'

'Yeah. And he started going around naked.'

'Naked?'

'Starkers. And worst of all, he said it was for my benefit. Said I had problems undressing. I mean, in front of other people. I won't play sport, you see. Not since they started this showering business. You have to go in all together.'

'In the altogether, is it?'

'Yeah, that sort of thing. I mean, it's not decent. My mother told me. And when I explained to him about this showering business, all he does is go and buy me a new towel. It had the word "SPORT" written on it. In capitals. I mean. That's the sort of person he is. Unreliable. And the house is a disaster. He won't let Uncle Frank even visit any more.' I could sense that I was losing the priest's attention. But I continued on. I needed to talk. 'Can you imagine? My father thinks he's going to make it into a boarding-house. I mean, who in their right mind'd want to stay there?'

'I might have to move in myself,' said Father Mulcahy darkly.

'What?'

'There's folk after my bollocks here, you know. New priests coming up, wanting promotion. The parish priest himself. Do anything to get rid of me. Out of the way, like.' He lit a cigarette. 'I've no stomach for this today,' he said.

'Can I put my glasses on, so?'

'Go on.'

He was pulling heavily on his Woodbine. With all the nicotine on his fingers, it looked like his smoking-hand wore a yellow glove.

'I buried your mother,' he said unexpectedly.

I could think of nothing to say, beyond, 'Thank you.'

'What harm?' he remarked. 'All in a day's work.'

He stubbed out his cigarette, squashing the butt and scraping it along a worn tin ashtray that said 'Britvic.'

I wondered if I liked him.

On the way home, bloody Mrs Houlihan stopped me again.

'Poor lamb,' she said. ''Tis shocking news.'

'What's shocking news?'

'Sure, I saw the ambulance and all.'

Her earrings were dangling away, and her smile was everlasting as usual. She really could be mistaken for a gypsy.

'Mrs Houlihan,' I said, 'I'm sick of this street and anxious for home. If you've something to tell me, just say it.'

'And I'm the last one now,' she said. 'All the others have left. Turfed out. I'm the last one now in the street. It's just you and me, now.'

The words she was speaking sounded like a complaint, or sounded at least like her voice should be sorrowful. But she was smiling gloriously away. Then she actually laughed. Uproariously.

'But I'll tell you what. I'll pop in now and then, and see to your belly. Okey-dokey, I know what a young man wants. I'll see to your belly. Now that your father's away.'

'He's away?'

She cackled an extra-uproarious laugh.

My Aunt Agnes was waiting for me in the sitting-room when I got home. My father had suffered his second stroke.

'Now Nilus,' said my Aunt Agnes, 'while your father's in hospital, I want you to know, you won't be alone. We'll be popping in, either me or your Uncle Frank. I'll bring your meals. Anything you want, just let me know. Don't be shy.'

'Thank you,' I said. I felt strange, out of place. We were in the sitting-room. We never used the sitting-room. Since my mother died. I was surprised it was still habitable.

'Now, would you like some soup?'

It was half-past four in the afternoon. 'For dinner?'

'No, no,' said my Aunt Agnes. 'We'll be eating here with you tonight. But we don't eat dinner till late, I'm afraid, your uncle and I. Sometimes as late as seven, seven-thirty. I mean, would you like some soup now?'.

I didn't know what all the fuss was about. I was quite capable of looking after myself. I always cooked the meals at home. The one time, after my mother's death, that my father tried his hand in the kitchen, I'd been served up some sort of mucously virescent doughy stuff. '*Pasta verde*,' my father had accounced triumphantly.

'I think I'm all right.'

'Are you sure?' my aunt persisted. 'If you're hungry I can put some soup on. No trouble at all. I brought some packets with me. But I don't want to spoil your appetite. So could you eat soup now and still manage your dinner after? What do you think?'

'I'm not hungry.' Then I considered that was a bit brusque, so I added, 'I had my sandwiches at school.'

'Sandwiches?'

'Yes.'

'Sandwiches don't sound very filling.'

My uncle came in with a newspaper.

'By the way,' she said, conspiratorially, 'your Uncle Frank was sitting in that armchair.'

I stood up.

'No, don't get up,' she said, flapping about.

'What's this?' said my uncle, sitting down on the sofa.

'He won't eat anything,' said my aunt.

'Maybe he's not hungry.' He opened out the paper and started to read. 'Well, sit down, Nilus. It's still your home.'

I sat down in the other armchair. My Aunt Agnes watched me for a moment. I had a feeling she was going to tell me she had been sitting there. But she didn't. She said, 'I think I'll put some soup on just in case.'

'He might not want it,' said my uncle.

'When it's ready he might feel like some.'

'If he wanted soup he'd tell us, wouldn't he?'

'I don't know. He might feel embarrassed.'

'Well, ask him. He's there. Do you want soup?'

I was already sick of this. There was no telling how long it might go on. To get it over with, I said, 'Yes, I want some soup.'

'See,' said my Aunt Agnes, exultantly. 'I knew he was hungry.' And she disappeared into the kitchen.

My uncle peeped out from behind his paper. 'Don't be bossed by her, Nilus. We men have to stick together. besides, she's a heart of gold underneath.' He leaned back on the sofa. 'Just been taking a look-see upstairs. No wonder your father had his second stroke. There's hammering and plastering and God knows what else done since last I was here. No wonder he's in hospital. I warned him.' He leaned closer towards me. 'By the way, Nilus. That chair you're sitting in. Your Aunt Agnes likes a soft cushion. She was sitting there.'

I got up and made my difficult way through the rubble and dilapidation to my bedroom. On the topmost landing, outside my bedroom door, I stopped and turned. The evening sun was shining through the west window. Its beams looked like columns, columns of dust and powdering plaster.

My uncle's business was so successful it seemed he could take as much time off work as he liked – worse luck. He took the opportunity of my father's hospitalization to visit me nearly every single afternoon and lecture me.

'You know, Nilus, I used to be a bit of a dreamer myself. When I was your age.' He looked at me. 'How old are you now?'

'Fourteen.'

'Fourteen? I thought you were older. Well no, then. I was older than you. I was nearly married. But I was a dreamer none the less.'

He stared off into space for a moment. I wondered was he practising a quick dream before he recommenced his lecturing.

'My dreaming, of course, took the form of politics. You might think that more useful than just moping around the day long. But no, it was still dreaming. Castles in the air.'

I was thinking about my jigsaw. Uncle Frank had caught me half-way through a game of Disturbance. The pieces were still lying up in my room in their jumble. I couldn't concentrate for worrying about them.

My uncle was going on about something. 'Burying our heads in the sand,' he said. 'I don't wish to appear cynical. God knows, we're all entitled to a dream or two. I was quite a fighter in those days, you know. We were all going to change the world. And we believed it. Meetings, rallies, shouting down rivals at factory gates, slogans. The whole shooting gallery.'

Worse, the beautiful square of flat matt black surface was lying up there disrupted, while I had to sit through this rigmarole.

'What did we achieve? Nothing. Mind you, I don't wish to take away a man's dreams, Nilus. I'm the last man. I won't deny it; I quite enjoyed myself. I still vote Labour. That might surprise you. But I still vote Labour. I'm not the hard-hat, hard-headed old army major they might make me out to be. But –' he tapped a pen on the coffee table, 'Where's the bottom line, I ask myself. As the Americans might say: where's the bottom line?'

I was worried about his pen. He was tapping it, point down, on the varnish on the table. My mother had varnished that table.

'Those days,' my uncle continued, 'well, they were good days. No matter what folk might say.'

I was far too disturbed with the pen on the varnish even to pretend to pay attention. 'Uncle Frank,' I said.

'Yes?'

I had no idea what to say – that would be at all relevant to his tirade. 'That pen,' I said, fairly desperately.

'Pen?' He glanced at his biro in his fingers. It said 'Moore's Construction'. When he twisted it, the reverse announced, 'Moore's Demolition'. 'Well?' said my uncle.

'I wondered if I might borrow it.'

He threw me his usual odd look.

I ruffled some sheets of paper that must have lain on the coffee table for aeons. 'To take notes,' I said. 'I don't want to miss anything.'

That pleased him. He handed me the pen. The coffee table was saved.

'Well, Nilus,' he resumed. 'Where was I?'

I was about to say that I was worried about my father, my home, but he found his train of thought too quickly for me.

'Those days – well, they were good days. No matter what folk might say. But Agnes – well, you get married. It's not easy when you have a wife and a baby daughter to support. You can't eat pamphlets, as she used say. Though God knows, I'm still a Labour man. I'm still up there with them. But – well, you know Agnes.' He considered this a moment, his usual aeon. Then: 'Yes, God knows where I'd be without her. It's entirely on account of her that I've got to where I am today. Entirely. Are you with me?'

I was remembering, I didn't know why, the giant picture windows they had in their sitting-room, way up on the Hill. You could stare hours on end through them at the tide on Killiney Bay.

'I think so,' I said.

'Good. Now. Take your father, for instance. I don't wish to speak ill of the sick, but what a time-waster! And he got this house and all! No application, that's his problem. Stuck in the old ways. Does he work, your father? 'Course he doesn't work. And where d'you think he gets his money? Who d'you think is shoring up this pile of old bricks? Some joker or other. Some muggins. We're not talking voting Labour here. We're talking business. He's a walking disaster, your father. He's living in the past. And if he thinks he's going to stand in my way, in the way of all decent progress, well. No disrespect, of course . . .'

37

Et cetera.

I rarely had a moment's peace. There was always one or the other of them popping in with either food or a lecture. Worse, there was no rhythm. 'Now Nilus, tell me,' my Aunt Agnes would say, 'what kinds of food do you not like to eat? Not a vegetarian or anything funny like that, are you? I remember when Ira was a vegetarian. Oh, we did laugh. Didn't we, Frankie?'

Then my uncle would get irritated because she kept interrupting his lectures and he'd say, 'Look, the boy'll eat anything. Custard and kippers, venison blancmange, anything you care to put in front of him. All right?'

'Well, I'm very glad to hear that. But we shan't be having venison, Frankie. The butcher doesn't stock it. And anyway I keep thinking of those poor deers. Or is it calves?'

I had always liked my Uncle Frank, and I'd never disliked my aunt. I just wished they'd leave me alone. I sat hours on end in my bedroom, witnessing the rain drive against the window. I had brought an electric fire up. It was calm in the dry heat, and the condensation slowly dribbling down the panes.

I played Disturbance.

When Mrs Houlihan had given me the jigsaw, a month or so before my mother died, she'd said, 'Poor lamb, it'll take your mind off things.'

I'd looked at the box she handed me in some surprise. It was plain black cardboard, in the shape of a shoe-box, with no writing on it, not even a picture. I didn't like touching it. You could never be sure of things out of these tradesmen-like cottages. My mother had told me that. Mrs Houlihan patted me on my head. I flinched.

''Tis only an oul' jigsaw,' she said.

As usual, I was sick of the street and anxious for home. That's probably why I didn't throw it back in her face. I ran home and carried the box straight up to my bedroom. There I promptly forgot about it. Another hideous sight had greeted me, as catastrophic as the chipped crockery: my mother hadn't made my bed.

It was only when my mother took to her bed, in her last confinement, and the crockery on the dresser could be disturbed no further, that I remembered the jigsaw. I lifted the lid off the black shoe-box and was amazed to find the myriad tiny black pieces inside. And they were all black. It was like no jigsaw puzzle I'd ever seen before: I put the lid back on, lay down on my bed, my nose turned up and the extremities of my mouth all crooked.

But I couldn't get the jigsaw out of my mind. I kept thinking of all those thousands of tiny black pieces and the disarray, the confusion of them, in that box. I couldn't get it out of my mind. Not just their image. It was almost the *feel* of them that antagonized me. All those pieces crying out for arrangement, for order. To *be* something.

I stole off my bed. I picked up my table, carried it and the jigsaw, still in its shoe-box, down the difficult stairs from the garret, into my mother's bedroom. Then I began.

It wasn't a pleasure to work on, the black jigsaw, though I worked at it like a demon, till late every night. Something about the jagged corners of the bit I had done, and the empty spaces inside, enraged me, ragged my sensibilities. I could barely stomach the sight of it, or the poor pieces in their jumble, pleading for meaning.

My mother moaned in her sleep. She had difficulty breathing. Sometimes, she needed to battle for her breath. At other times, her breath was barely detectable, like a tide on an inland sea. And as the flat matt black surface pervaded more and more of the empty space, I came to identify the jigsaw with her labour. It was nonsense, of course. I was tired. But I began to think that it was me and my driven need to complete the jigsaw that was killing my mother. With every piece I positioned, I blocked out another space for her to breathe. I was suffocating her.

I knew I couldn't live with the puzzle unfinished in the house, so I toyed with the idea of throwing the whole thing away, of burning it, burying it, whatever.

And while I toyed with these ideas, concocting elaborate methods of achieving them, I continued placing the tiny black pieces together.

My mother was fading obviously now, hour by hour. It wouldn't be long. The jigsaw was nearly finished. Then, when I was down to my last hundred or so pieces, a spark of hope came to lighten my secret darkness. There was one corner piece missing. I could see. It wasn't there. I worked feverishly for an hour, till I had used up all the pieces remaining. I sat back in some relief, if not triumph. The jigsaw puzzle had come to me with one piece missing. The fourth corner piece, on the bottom right-hand side. Fate had taken a hand.

There was a rustle from my mother's bed. I looked up. She was awake. She called me.

'Nilus,' she said. She touched my hand. I held hers in mine. We had held hands so many times. I knew the wrinkles of her palm like I knew the phases of the moon. But her hand had suffered. I could have been holding a glove.

She died the next day.

I came home from school, that Monday, that next day, a year ago. I went up to my mother's room. I didn't need to look at her. The jigsaw told me.

'I found the missing piece,' said my father. 'It had slipped under the bed.'

40

I didn't cry. Some things are too critical for tears. I looked at my mother. She was neat in her bed. Her eyes were placidly watching the cracks on the ceiling, as though reading there directions on a heavenly chart. One foot hung out of the bed. Perhaps at her last she had sought to thwart my father's folly. Eyes on the ceiling, one foot to the floor; her body stiffening between.

One evening, my Uncle Frank found me in my bedroom. He didn't seem annoyed. Didn't start on at me about dreaming or moping around the day long. He said, 'Well Nilus, your father's due out of hospital tomorrow. I thought we'd take this opportunity for a last little chat.'

He sat down heavily on the edge of my bed. I had stood up when he entered. Now I sat down near him, choosing a straight-back chair. It seemed appropriate. He said nothing for a while, and together we stared at the rain against the window panes. Then he brightened. 'You know that swimming-pool I have in the grounds at home?'

'Yes.'

'You know why it's in the shape of an N?'

I shook my head.

'The man who had my house before me had it built that way. To remind him of his late wife.' A smile flickered on his face, as if he was touched by the man's devotion.

'I see,' I said, though why an odd-shaped pool should remind someone of his dead wife I couldn't make out.

'Her name was Nora, of course,' he said, almost snapping.

'Yes,' I answered quickly. 'Nora. Yes, of course.'

He took in a biggish breath. 'When I bought the house, I promised your aunt I'd have the pool reshaped to an A.'

The condensation from the damp air round the electric

41

fire was curling up the inside of my glasses. I tried to wipe the lenses without taking them off. I was anxious not to appear inattentive.

'A for Agnes, of course,' said my uncle. He paused for a while, unsure where to go on from there. He looked around him. I presumed he saw the neatness of my room. 'But could you imagine the mess?' he asked. 'The unnecessary expense? Workmen trooping in and out? Excavations, fillings-in?'

I nodded my head vigorously. I could imagine the mess only too well.

'After all, as a pool for swimming in it's perfectly adequate. Whatever the shape. The problem had me perplexed a long time. Until last night, that is. When the solution came to me like a bolt from the blue.'

He stopped again. I wondered if he wanted me to ask a question. 'What was the solution?' I asked.

But he didn't answer that. 'You see, Nilus,' he said, 'I don't want to drive a wedge between father and son. Of course I don't. I'm the last man. But you've got to make him see sense. I'm not after a civil war. It's for his own benefit, God damn it. Where's the future in this old shambles? It's business. Common business sense. Like I've been telling you, Nilus.'

He stood up. I had a feeling the edge of the bed was too comfortable for what he had to say. He zig-zagged about my bedroom, making wide collecting gestures with his hands.

'Why d'you think I own a dream house on Killiney Hill with a swimming-pool, three cars, what have you? That didn't arrive from nowhere. All that didn't just arrive one day in a nice package with a ribbon on the top and a message saying "Birthday Greetings from Your Loving God". I had to work for that and work damn bloody hard.' He sat down. 'Your aunt too.' He stood up. 'Your mother, God bless her soul and all that, gave in. Your father defeated her. The imbecile. She gave in and gave up. Your father's an imbecile, a joker. A loser. God knows, he doesn't even vote Labour, but he's worried about the cottages.' He sat down again. 'I have a terrible fear you might be going the same way. I do.' He stood up. 'You've got to pull your socks up. It's make your mind up time. It's now or never. You've got to stop this dreaming and moping about in your bedroom. Your mother's dead. Open your eyes. It's business I'm talking.'

He said some more things. I wasn't listening. I was worrying had he disturbed the sheet-folds of my bed with all his leaping up and collapsing down.

My uncle had finished his lecture. I knew this because he was giving me a long searching look. I blinked. It seemed polite.

'Dinner's at seven,' he said. 'Ira's coming with that joker boyfriend of hers.'

'Coming here?'

'I was born here, you know. Probably the last meal I'll eat here. I'm not sentimental, but that must stand for something. Your Auntie Nessie is bringing the food. She's cooking up something special.'

'Who's my Auntie Nessie?'

'Oh. Did I not tell you? I decided last night I'd leave the swimming-pool the way it is. I decided we'd change your aunt's name instead. A for Agnes, but N for your Auntie Nessie.'

All through dinner, I couldn't take my eyes off my aunt. If

ever there was an Agnes, it was she. She wore old tweedy things and, when she was outside, hats with the brim at the back and see-through plastic raincoats. She was an Agnes.

Except now, everybody – even her daughter's boyfriend – was calling her Nessie. Such power my uncle wielded; I was awestruck. He didn't seem to mind – probably didn't even notice – the disorder he wreaked.

My cousin Ira was late for the meal. She breezed in, kissed her father on the forehead, then said to me, 'Nilus! Haven't seen you since antebellum.'

Auntie Bellum, I thought. Who the hell is she? I was that agitated. In the time before death and illness and my father's raging rows with my uncle, our families had spent a week together every year on the sands in Courtown. Ira used kick sand in my face, then. I wondered was she doing the same now, metaphorically.

She was about twenty years old. Her boyfriend was an ugly tradesman-like fellow. He had thick hair and dunga-rees. My uncle called him 'that joker', and my aunt called him 'Ira's beau'. Neither of them could remember his name.

We ate dinner in the dining-room. When I'd found out my new Auntie Nessie intended to serve the food there, I'd confronted her, hands on my hip. 'We can't eat there,' I said.

'Why not?'

'The rubble,' I said. 'All the tiles hanging from the ceil-ing. The wallpaper peeling. The damp.'

But when she opened the door, I was dumbfounded.

'It's a bit dusty,' she said. 'Obviously no one's been in for a while. But I can't see any rubble.'

I was amazed. She was wrong about nobody being in. My father must have worked like a demon out of hell to get the place in that shape.

Dinner itself passed reasonably enough. It was only afterwards that the fireworks began.

'You enjoy that, Frankie?' my aunt said. 'It was your favourite.'

'Lovely, Nessie. Wonderful.'

'No reservations?'

'None at all.' He stuck a finger up from the back of his head, and made a squawking 'brave's' noise, with his other hand beating against his mouth. 'I'm like a Red Indian. No reservations at all.'

'You're in a good mood, Daddy,' said Ira.

'And why not?'

She leaned across the table. She had been drinking wine. 'Daddy, Joe's going on a trip tomorrow. He's going up North.'

'Don't tell me, I don't want to know.'

There was a sudden silence at the table. My uncle was glaring at his plate and Joe was glaring at Ira and Ira was smiling at her wine glass, twisting it in her hand.

My new Auntie Nessie came back from the kitchen. She was humming a hymn. 'The day Thou gavest Lord hath ended'. She gazed around the table, smiling at everybody, then sat down in an armchair in the recess. She picked up a magazine.

'Was that a visitation?' said my Uncle Frank, regaining his spirits somewhat.

'A portent of good or evil?' chimed in Ira.

'No, it was just your mother after being at the sherry bottle.'

'Now, I can hear what you're saying over there,' she called.

'So tell me, young joker,' said Uncle Frank to Ira's beau, the first words he'd addressed to him all evening, 'what's this holiday in the North in aid of?'

45

The joker coughed. 'It's – er – well, you see – it's – er – not really –'

'I didn't think you were taking the tourist trail to Belfast.'

'Go on, Joe. Tell him what you told me.' This was Ira.

'Let him speak for himself,' said my uncle.

'I didn't say anything.'

'It's only that the comra – I mean, the committee – you know, gesture of support, like –' He had the same trades-man-like accent as his looks. 'The concer – cer – certed effort of the working class,' he said.

'Would anyone like a chocolate?' called my aunt from her recess.

'I'm only going as a gesture – you know – of solidarity – brother – brotherhood, like –'

'That's wonderful. You're all all right, folks. You've got the brotherhood of Joe Joker behind you.'

'Nilus,' said Auntie Nessie, 'be a good boy and ask your uncle would he like a chocolate.'

'Smile everyone. Say cheese. You've got the solidarity of Joe Joker behind you.'

'Uncle Frank,' I said, but he was in full flow.

'Everything's coming up roses,' he continued. 'Captain Joe Joker's at the helm.'

'It's just with the – you know – concer – cer – cer – blast it! The *concerted* effort of the – er – er –'

'You mean bombing the hell out of people? Are you apologizing for that crowd now? Those people up there are reasonably ordinary folk, you know. People with their initials on their coffee cups. They're not aliens. I've got bloody working factories up there. In between the smith-ereens of your chaps' carry-on.'

'It's a – it's a war – of liber – you know, liberation –'

'Don't give me that crap. Last time I was up there, I

46

couldn't order a whiskey without choosing between Scotch and Irish. I couldn't walk the streets without your crowd of bootboys stopping me, ordering me at the point of a knife to recite the Hail Mary. You're an ignorant dreamer, son. Worse than this boy's father.'

'Go on, Nilus,' said my aunt. 'See if he'd like a chocolate.'

'Uncle Frank?' I said.

'What is it?'

I was hating this. I hadn't expected this. 'Aunt Agnes –' I swallowed. I was worried he might mistake my stumbling for the joker. 'I mean, my Auntie Nessie – she wants to know if you want a chocolate.'

'What's wrong with you, Nessie? You want another sherry? Will someone please fetch Nessie another sherry.'

'No I don't want another sherry. You're just trying to get me tipsy, I know.'

'I think she's made a good enough job of that herself,' said Ira.

'Where was I?' said my uncle.

'Reciting the Hail Mary at the point of a knife,' said Ira, helpfully.

'In a – in a – you know – proletariat revolution, mistakes do happen. We're not in – in – in – like the Pope –'

'Infallible,' said Ira.

'Infallible. We're not in – but that doesn't mean we should give up – like Lenin said – the struggle for social – and Connolly too – for social – and it happened the same in Russia –'

'You never finish what you're bloody saying. I know your sort. You go on and on about concercercercerted effort and in the meantime my workers are losing wages. I'm losing business.'

'But Daddy, you were a socialist once. You say you still vote Labour.'

'Yeah,' said the joker. 'And at least I'm doing something. Not sitting on me backside making excuses the day long.'

'You spoke a whole sentence,' said Ira, grinning nicely at her beau.

My uncle had leaped to his feet by now. 'Doing something? You? You want to get a job, you do. You want to get a taste of the real world. Think she'll marry you?' He was pointing at Ira. His finger wagged oddly at the end of his stiffened arm. 'Think she'll want to traipse around after the likes of you? With a baby in her arms? You've no right giving her a baby at all. You? You haven't two pennies to rub together even!'

'It's just that we decided – like – we wanted the sound of – pattering – er – pattering – er – pattering – er –'

'I'll tell you what –' began my uncle.

'Dammit! Children!' The joker spat out the word.

'Child,' Ira corrected him.

'I'll tell you what,' my uncle repeated. 'When you wipe the milk of your precious Connolly off of your chin, then I'll listen to you. Until then, you keep a-bloody-way!' He stormed out of the dining-room.

'Frank?' called my aunt, running after him. 'Frankie!'

Ira took another swigful from her glass, emptying it. She half-filled it again with the dregs from the wine bottle, downed that. 'I knew it'd be a good show,' she said. 'Never fails.'

'Next time,' said the joker, 'you can come to dinner on your own. You always push him, you do. Egg him on.' It was interesting to notice that the joker lost all trace of a stammer when my uncle was out of the room.

'Doesn't look like there'll be another time,' said Ira. 'Well, little Nilus. What d'you make of it all?'

'Me?' I said. I thought my home was bad enough with

48

just my father and his manias. With them here it was impossible. I wanted none of this. 'I don't know.'

'Know something, Nilus? I like you. I've always liked you. You're the only person I could ever feel totally alone with.'

She was drunk.

'You coming home?' said the joker.

'No, I'm staying with Daddy tonight.'

The joker hesitated a moment. 'Daddy?' he said, pronouncing the word very unattractively.

'Daddy,' she confirmed.

'All right,' he said. 'All right.' He shrugged. He sat down for a while, like he hadn't shrugged. Then he said again, 'You coming home?'

'No.'

He stood up. 'Ira?'

'No, Joe.'

'All right then.' And he sloped off.

'I'm sick of the lot of them,' said Ira, as if I was interested enough to require an explanation. 'I thought we were going to get married. You know that? Married . . . Married,' she repeated. Her grin could be so unpleasant. 'Married! He doesn't want a wife. All he wants is a footslog to hand out his pamphlets for him.' She dregged her wine. 'I'm going to speak to Daddy. He understands.'

'I thought he was one of your socialists.'

'Daddy?' She stopped by the door.

I wished I'd kept my big mouth shut. I'd delayed her, and now it looked like I'd have to find some way of making my comment sound reasonable. 'Keeps going on about voting Labour or something,' I mumbled to my place mat.

'Daddy's all talk. Mummy saw to that.'

She went. Phew, I thought.

49

After she'd gone, my new Auntie Nessie came in, sniffing back some tears. 'Nilus, why oh why?' she wanted to know. 'Why can't they just stop it? It's all such nonsense. We haven't a shred of common Christian courtesy. Why?'

'Yes,' I said. I was embarrassed. I suppose she could as well have been talking to a lamp-post. Then I remembered her sherry bottle. 'Hold on a second. I'll fetch you something.'

I found her bottle in the kitchen, poured her a glass. I was praying this awful day might be over now and I could go to my room. 'Here you are,' I said.

'Sherry? What's that for?'

'I thought you needed it.'

'Nonsense.' She had regained her composure so thoroughly, it was as if she'd never cried in her life.

'But I –'

'Nonsense. You can't drink away your sorrows, Nilus. You'll have to learn that. Now, it'll soon be time for supper, and with Ira coming home I wonder if she'd like a glass of milk now or would she prefer to wait till . . .'

She wandered out of the dining-room again. I knocked the glass of sherry back in one go. Then spat it out. I'd poured from the vinegar bottle by mistake.

The ambulance drove off. I stood on the driveway and watched my father climb slowly up the steps to the porch. 'Hello Nilus,' was all he had said to me. He had always been lean. But now his face looked spare, the colour and composition of a pencil portrait. He was still my father, except he looked like someone had drawn a portrait of him, three weeks before, but had run out of pencil half-way through.

It began to rain. It took him a long time to climb the steps. I watched him through the drizzle. He looked like a character at the end of a film. For all his effort he never seemed to make very much progress. The dilapidated scenery moved with him.

They had given me his belongings to carry. The bag was open. Placed on top there was a framed photograph of my mother. The rain splattered on it. She was in her celeste cardigan. She had her long hair caught in her ribbon. Already I'd forgotten the exact colour. She was smiling. Although, of course, I knew who she was, it was difficult actually to recognize her.

I realized suddenly that it wasn't a picture of my mother at all. It was a picture of his wife.

He was still on the steps. 'Dad,' I called.

Nothing.

'Dad, wait for me.'

I suppose anybody else would have found the house gloomy after that. But I savoured the quiet. I had time and latitude to get on with Disturbance and perfect the sheet-folds of my bed. I went to school in the morning and came home in the evening. After the disproportionate comings of my uncle and aunt, I was busy with routine.

My father took to his bed. In the night-time before I went myself to bed, I would visit him to see if he lacked for anything. But he was always too weak, too exhausted with the length of the day, or the speed of the ticking clock, to speak much. Sometimes I couldn't bear even to enter his room. I just stood in the jar of the door, and listened to his troubled, croaking breath. There was always a glass of medicine at his side, and I would watch his trembling fingers reach out to grasp it.

I'd creep back to my room then and crawl into my bed.

Sometimes I'd get up in the middle of the night and take out the letters from my locked cabinet beside my jigsaw and read them again. These were letters my father had written to my mother, a long time ago. He didn't know I had them, though it was he who'd given them to me. I suppose it was a mistake, but such bungling carelessness alarmed me almost as much as their content.

I could remember the night he gave me the letters. We were in his bedroom. He was changing his clothes, I think, and I was delaying my bedtime. I was pestering him for paper. I'd just learned my alphabet. I wanted to practise. I nagged so much that eventually he gave in. He tried the drawers of his own chest first, but finding nothing there, he opened the top drawer of my mother's dressing-table, her jewellery drawer. He took a sheaf of old papers out, leafed through them lackadaisically. 'Here you are,' he said. 'The backs haven't been used. You can try your alphabet on the back – but only if you go to bed – *now!*'

I went to bed. My father soon forgot all about the letters. I kept them for scribbling on. Until I learned to read joined-up handwriting. Then I practised my reading on their written sides.

Their content only dawned on me slowly. That's probably why I never grew to hate my father, only to distrust him. It's a wonder. It's not easy reading letters from your father to your mother, begging her to murder you.

And now my father was dying. I'd always had difficulty with him, with his whims and sudden enthusiasms. Only my mother had kept him in check. Now he was going to meet her again. I had difficulty knowing how I felt about that.

Except one thing was for certain: I couldn't stand even the notion of my Uncle Frank and my Auntie Nessie adopting me.

'Leave your glasses on,' said Father Mulcahy wearily. 'I've no stomach for portraiture today.'

He took out his crumpled packet of Woodbines. He stared at the cigarettes as if unable to decide which one to smoke.

'Were you ever,' he said, 'tempted to take a gasper?'

I was shocked. 'Of course not,' I said. 'I'm far too young.'

He eyed me crookedly. His mouth twisted to the usual distaste. He said, 'I was smoking at your age.'

'But I don't want to smoke.'

'Then why didn't you just say that?'

I tried to formulate reasons. Nothing very intelligent would come out. I just shrugged.

'That bloody Father lick-the-bishop's-arse Mooney has been at me again,' he muttered, almost to himself. He was off once more. 'Wouldn't you think a Christian soul'd leave a man in peace a few years? A decent retirement, I might have. But no. He wants me out. Any excuse. There's moves afoot to cart me off to the Missions. Not me. I've no taste for piccaninnies.'

He continued on in the same vein. I scanned around his room. It had its plus points. It was clean and it was tidy. But it was terribly bare. The only objects of any personality were the sketches of four churches he had framed and hung on his walls. They were the four churches he had served in. I found them unattractive. I could do without his personality. It was like if you suddenly found Adam or Eve without their fig leaves on.

I didn't know why I kept on visiting him. There was always the same rigmarole about glasses and riff-raff. But I was no closer to becoming an altar boy. I couldn't work out whether to be pleased or distressed.

'My father's ill in his bed,' I said. 'He won't let my Uncle Frank visit. Still. "Don't ever darken my door again," he said to him. I think he's going to die.'

But Father Mulcahy had other things on his mind. 'Them bastards. They won't even allow me altar boys now.' He lowered his head sadly. 'And I used to enjoy my altar boys. So I did.'

He'd obviously been drinking. I left him to it. I had no

particular feelings for him, one way or the other. I just enjoyed having somewhere to go, something to do. That was all.

Outside, I watched a beggar-type person shuffling up the steps to the church. He was dragging a battered heavy case with him. The case annoyed me. It was unpleasantly, irregularly quadrangular, as if it couldn't make up its mind to be a square or a triangle. At the top of the steps he set this case down, felt around its top end, fingering for the locks. I understood he was blind. He looked vaguely familiar.

He took out a piano accordion, heaved it to his shoulders. There was a jangle of mis-struck chords. As I walked past, he called out, 'Name the tune, any tune, I'll play it. Any tune at all. No jigs or reels, mind. No jigs or reels.' Then, specifically to me, 'You, young man, what tune would you like?'

'I thought you were blind,' I said.

'It's Niall Moore, isn't it?'

I recognized him then. He used to live in one of the cottages in our street, before my uncle had wrangled the deeds from my father, turfed him out. I gave him some money, and when he insisted on playing me a tune, I chose 'Nobody's Child'.

All the way home, through the stranded, bereft streets, the song was in my ears.

> *No mummy's kisses*
> *And no daddy's smiles,*
> *Nobody wants me,*
> *I'm nobody's child.*

Such maudlin words. I had no idea why I'd chosen it. My mother was dead and my father was dying. That's all I knew.

On the way home, I saw there was a salt-of-the-earth man hammering boards on to Mrs Houlihan's windows. At first I sniggered. She can't afford curtains for the night, I thought. Then I considered she might find daytime rather dim. I stopped outside the door.

'Where's Mrs Houlihan?' I demanded.

'Gone,' said the man.

'Gone where?'

'Turfed out.'

'What d'you mean, turfed out?'

The man inspected me with his dulling salt-of-the-earth eyes. 'Who's asking?' he said.

I hurried home, busy with this news. Mrs Houlihan had given up. Now my father and I had the whole street to ourselves.

As soon as I got in, I knew for certain there was nobody home. I didn't know how I knew, but I was certain of what had happened. My father had died.

I decided to visit my father's room, to see if they'd carted away his dead body. When I was half-way up the stairs, it occurred to me that I was walking on tip-toe. I stopped.

'I am stilled by a rare silence,' I said, then wondered why I'd said it. After a moment I was convinced somebody else had spoken. I turned, but of course there was nobody there. A notion struck me that I was the only person left in the world. There was a word that described this feeling. I tried to remember it. Something like 'brainchill'. Was that it? Brainchill? There was nothing for it but to dash up to my bedroom and check through my dictionary. I didn't. I tip-toed.

I was touching unparticular objects – mouldings, door-knobs – all made extraordinary by my aloneness. I needed reassurance. But also there was a side to my brain that was quietly amazed that the house continued – in bricks and mortar – when my father was dead. It seemed an extraordinary extravagance, given the poor mouth he sometimes affected. I felt I was on the verge of a dreadful discovery. Then I remembered it had already happened. Or had it? The tension twisted in my head. 'Migraine,' I said, then hurried on before I could doubt I'd said it.

'Brainchill,' I said again. I'd looked it up, but there was no such word in my dictionary. I sat down on my bed, fingering the coverlet. I knew of a sudden that I was about to cry, and to dam this I reached under the mattress to check the sheet-folds. Everything was correct. I took my glasses off to polish them on my jumper. But I ended up smearing them with my fingers by mistake. I giggled at my silliness and at the same time wiped a tear from my eye.

There was nothing to do in my bedroom. I decided to go downstairs again. This time I started running. I dashed down the stairs, two, three at a time. I thrust myself into the kitchen, shouting, 'Dad! Come back!' Except what came out didn't sound at all like that. It sounded like 'Dad! You bastard!'

The force of my entry dissipated. I looked idly around. Then I saw there was someone else in the kitchen. I couldn't believe it. It was monstrous. She was doing something with the dresser.

'What're you doing with the dresser?' I demanded.

She turned, faced me. 'Is it you, poor lamb? You're home so.'

It was Mrs Houlihan.

I had to sit down. The shock of the dresser was almost too much for me.

'Poor lamb,' said Mrs Houlihan again. She had made a

pot of tea. She fetched me a cup from the dresser. 'Okey-dokey, plenty of sugar,' she said. 'Good strong sweet tea. That's what a young man needs.'

I tried to say something. All that would come out, in a sort of croaking, onomatopoeic voice, was, 'The crockery . . .'

She turned to view her handiwork. 'What d'you think?'

I forced myself to look at the dresser. There gleaming on the shelves, arrayed like wedding presents for a queen, were all the old cups and the saucers, all gleaming whiter than ever I could remember, without a chip, a crack, without even a scrape between them.

For a moment I had a vision of my mother smiling in a new celeste cardigan with wind through her hair, in a heaven of shimmering porcelain. And my father coming towards her, dancing.

'Well,' said Mrs Houlihan, 'if it's a boarding-house we're aiming at, we'll need to keep a duster handy.'

'Boarding-house?' This was outlandish. 'And my father just dead?'

'Dead? What're you on about at all? Your Da's not dead.'

'He is!' I cried. 'He is!' I stamped my foot – I suppose, petulantly.

'Poor lamb, don't be acting the maggot. Haven't I only been speaking to him upstairs?'

'Upstairs?'

'He's in his bed, sure.'

I had to sit down. Brainchill, I said to myself. Brainchill. There were footsteps on the stairs. My father walked into the kitchen. He actually walked in. He took the kettle, filled it with water, glanced over his shoulder, saw me, 'Hello Nilus,' he said, placed the kettle on the hob, sat down, took up the paper. 'It wouldn't have done you any harm to bring me up a cup of tea yourself. You know I'm only out of hospital.'

I said nothing. When the tea was made my father ported his cup and saucer to the door. 'I'm off back to bed, Mrs Houlihan,' he said.

'Okey-dokey. Dinner won't be long.'

I listened to the familiar tread of his feet on the stairs.

Dead? He didn't even look ill.

I raced after him. He was already in his bed. 'I thought you were supposed to be dying!' I said. 'I thought you were dead!'

'And what gave you that idea?'

'I don't know,' I said. 'I don't know.' I tried to remember, but my brain was too busy. 'Why did you take to your bed so?'

'Listen to him,' said my father. 'If anyone took to his bed, it's you. I've hardly glimpsed you these last few weeks. When you're not delaying in school, you're hidden away in your room. What you find to get up to there, I don't know. The only time I see you is late at night, hanging about my door, waking me up. You won't even bring me my tray proper, but plonk it down on the washstand where I can't get at it. Then you disappear.'

Could this possibly be true?

He reached for his glass of medicine. It was empty. 'Pass me that bottle there.'

'What bottle?'

'The brandy bottle.'

Brandy? It wasn't even medicine he was taking. There was a smell lingering about him. It was a sweet smell – so sweet it was pungent. A draught caught it from the window, and made my nostrils wince. It was like distant onions rotting.

'What's that smell?'

'What smell is that?'

'The smell of rotting things. Coming from you. The smell of death.'

He thought a while, eyeing me queerly, 'That'll be the garlic,' he decided. 'Mrs Houlihan's feeding me up on garlic. Does wonders to your system. You should try some yourself, Nilus. You're looking a bit off-colour these days.'

He was throwing a knowing risus at me. His hand was proffering a clove of garlic. I turned around, and sought out Mrs Houlihan in the kitchen.

'I'm to do the cooking, sure,' said Mrs Houlihan. She smiled that silly smile of hers. 'Your Da's opening up for business, end of the month. A boarding-house. Won't that be nice and fitting?'

It occurred to me all I had to do was turn my back for one second, have my portrait done by a drunken priest, and the whole world was out of control.

'Okey-dokey,' said Mrs Houlihan. 'How's about our dinners? Boiled spuds and ham, that's what a young man likes. Boiled spuds and ham.'

I was about to tell her it was Wednesday, and on Wednesdays I always cooked bacon for dinner, not ham. But I desisted.

A cup of tea had arrived in front of me. I ran my finger along the edge of the cup. The rim had the smoothness of silk. It was as though chips and chipped crockery hadn't even been invented yet.

That evening, after dinner, Mrs Houlihan appeared to have a fit of trembling. 'Dear me,' she said. 'I'm getting an "een".'

I looked over at my father, but he was busy peeling a clove of garlic. We were dining in his bedroom. 'Celebration,' Mrs Houlihan had called it. I'd had to lug the table in.

'A definite "een",' Mrs Houlihan continued. 'Irene, is it?' She spoke to the air above her, as if addressing the electric light in the shape of a chandelier that hung above my father's bed.

I considered correcting her. 'The name "Irene" has three syllables,' I might have said. 'It's not an "een".'

She thwarted me.

'Doreen?' she enquired of the chandelier.

The cutlery in her hands was rattling away. She was gripping it very tightly. I couldn't tell whether her fingers were causing this rattling, or if she really was trying to steady it. 'Come on now,' she continued, slightly scoldingly at the electric chandelier. 'Don't be playing the boot. If you've something to say, spit it out.'

'Mrs Houlihan?' I said.

'*Maureen*,' she said, decidedly. 'Nice to meet you again.'

'Mrs Houlihan?'

'Quiet now,' said my father. He'd forgotten his garlic, and was watching her in earnest.

Mrs Houlihan had her ear cocked towards the electric chandelier, as if trying to catch some distant melody that chinked through the glass. 'Okey-dokey,' she said matter-of-factly, and immediately the rattling stopped. She turned to me and smiled. 'Your mother says not to worry. Everything's hunky-dory upstairs. But you're to clean your teeth after every meal.'

'Sound advice,' said my father.

I stood up. 'My mother's dead,' I said.

'Poor lamb, of course Maureen's dead. She'd tell you herself otherwise.'

'What're you playing at?'

Mrs Houlihan smiled that mawkish lingering ugly smile. Even when she stopped, the smile seemed still to be there, hanging aimless in the air.

My father looked slowly upwards. I followed his gaze. The electric chandelier hung high over his bed. I squinted. The light hurt my eyes.

'Did you not know?' said my father. 'Mrs Houlihan is a medium.'

'And d'you know why I'm a medium?' said Mrs Houlihan.

I shook my head carefully.

'Why, because I'm neither rare nor well-done.' She laughed uproariously, thrusting back her black locks of hair, so that the bull-nose rings on her ears jangled dizzily about.

I left my father's bedroom and headed straight for the landing bathroom. I stumbled, but in the dim light I couldn't make out was it new rubble or old that had tripped me. I closed the bathroom door after me. The complaint of its rusty hinges was still in my ears, even after I'd caught my breath.

I found my brush. Then I cleaned my teeth.

Nothing was said that night. I went to bed before Mrs Houlihan. But I knew as soon as I awoke the next morning that she'd stayed the night. As I dressed I wondered how I felt about this. Something had to be done. Or rather, something had to be said.

I found her in the kitchen.

'And aren't you the one up with the lark and no mistake,' she said. 'Sure, I haven't the bread baked yet.'

'Mrs Houlihan,' I said strictly, 'I want to know: will you be living in here?'

'And why wouldn't you ask your Da?'

My Da, as you call him, I considered telling her, is a murdering maniac and I've as much chance getting sense out of him as out of that dough you're kneading on the board there.

I didn't say anything. I watched her kneading the dough. Her hands were covered in flour. I wondered had she washed them. My mother had never baked bread. She had always bought bread in. Sliced pans. Mrs Houlihan's nimbleness held me. Her hands were big and her fingers left deep prints in the dough. But she moved precisely, delicately even. I tried to figure out what an instruction leaflet for this work would look like. It would be incredibly complicated and almost impossible to follow.

'And are you all ready for school?'

'Mrs Houlihan,' I said, again strictly, 'school is my affair.'

So she was there. For good, apparently. I didn't really object. She spent her time in the kitchen, mostly. And she soon had it sparkling span-new. The meals she prepared were always served on time – even if she did neglect my mother's old hebdomadal routine of ham on Mondays, chops on Tuesdays, bacon on Wednesdays, et cetera. I wasn't too put out.

Nothing much happened. Then one morning, I woke up to the sound of diesel engines. I dashed over to my window. There were bulldozers attacking Mrs Houlihan's old cottage.

I found her in the kitchen. She was washing up. The cutlery started up a tremendous rattling in her clutches.

'They're knocking down your old cottage,' I said, casually, testing the water.

'And don't I know it,' she replied, and for once she didn't overwhelm me with her cheerfulness. I was pleased of that. I needed a perspective for this news, and Mrs Houlihan's demeanour told me I was right to be concerned.

My father was no such help. I had been correct about one thing when I thought he was dying. He might not be bed-bound, but he was certainly spending longer and longer in his bed.

I brought him his breakfast.

'Oh, so you're feeding the ghost, is it?'

This was his joke.

I set his tray down. He sniffed at it. 'As fare for a ghost might go, it whiffs fairly substantial.'

'Dad,' I said, 'I really thought you were going to die.' I still felt cheated. I had actually cared about him, and he just took it as a joke.

'We're all of us going to die.' He laughed at this, a rather thin laugh. 'God preserve us.'

'What d'you do all the time you spend in your bed?'

'Do?'

'I mean, if you're not dying?'

'I lie here,' he chuckled, 'pondering on the futility of it all.'

It was obviously an enjoyable occupation because I had rarely seen his spirits so high. He was unpeeling a garlic. He took a clove and popped it in his mouth, chewed happily.

'There's a fierce stench,' I said. 'Of garlic.'

'Only because you don't eat it.'

I could have said, only because you *do* eat it. But that would just have produced a stalemate. I said, instead, 'They're knocking down Mrs Houlihan's cottage.'

He wasn't interested. 'I want you to go to the off-licence.'

'Off-licence?' My father had never been a drinker. A drop here and there, but we never had bottles in the house. Until he came out of hospital.

'I want a bottle of brandy. No, fetch me two bottles. Fetch me a case.'

The doctor had warned him, in his condition, to stay off the drink. If he did drink, he should stick to brandy. That was enough for my father. He took to tippling brandy morning, noon and night. He thought it was a wonderful joke. It was symptomatic of the change that had come over him. Everything was a joke now, an occasion for his thin laughter.

'I'm not fetching brandy,' I said. 'I have to go to school.'

I couldn't concentrate at school. I was worrying about the bulldozers, like on the annual holiday with Uncle Frank and his family, in our caravan on the sands at Courtown, I used to worry about the sea: what if the tide forgot to stop?

I walked home from school, dawdling the way, like a man I'd seen once in a cartoon who had chewing-gum stuck to his shoes. The workmen had gone by the time I got to our street. I studied Mrs Houlihan's ex-cottage.

They had left one wall standing. A dirty old curtain fluttered pointlessly from a window. The wall leaned at a difficult angle. I calculated the angle, for all the world like it was a problem at maths class. Was it sustainable? I doubted it.

I was glad they'd left one wall standing. It meant I didn't have to contend with a totally empty space in my notion of our street. At the same time, however, there was another side to my thinking, erosive and contrarious, that wished they'd knocked the whole thing down, swept it clean away. Then Mrs Houlihan's ex-cottage could have been just an empty space.

It was brainchill. I knew.

'The mark of a true vandal,' said Mrs Houlihan, later. 'Destruction isn't good enough, but they have to leave traces behind them of what was there before. To remind us.'

So I knew where she stood. 'I'm sure it's just that they didn't have time today,' I said, to comfort her. 'I'm sure they'll come back and finish knocking it down. Tomorrow, probably. Or Monday, if they don't work weekends.' She didn't seem very comforted, so I decided to change the subject. 'How's the boarding-house situation?'

'Coming along.' She did brighten a bit. 'Okey-dokey, hunky-dory. Won't be long now and we'll have our first guest.'

This was better news. My Uncle Frank knew what he'd been talking about. Idle buildings earning their keep, and all that. The cottages might belong to people who were the salt of the earth, but still they were being bulldozed away. I knew why. My uncle had told me. It was because they were idle. Because they served no purpose. Our house, of course, had never been idle. After all, it was my home. But you couldn't rest on your laurels. Opening it up as a boarding-house would double its purpose, and earn – maybe – some remuneration into the bargain.

'I have somebody in mind already,' she said.

'Mrs Houlihan,' I replied in genuine admiration, 'you must have a business brain.' I was remembering my Uncle Frank's last lecture to me.

She twisted her head to a canny position. Her four earrings banged against each other. 'Not so much a brain, as an instinct.'

On my way to bed, I brushed against an old cobweb trailing from the ceiling. Even the cobwebs were falling down now. The upstairs hall was filthy. Recently, what with my uncle and aunt and Mrs Houlihan's sudden arrival, I'd neglected to remember exactly how dilapidated it looked. Odd bits of wall had been scraped clean, odd bits of ceiling had been re-tiled. But these evidences of my father's scattered efforts of a month before lent the place, if anything, an even more dismal look. I shuddered.

There was nothing for it. First thing the next day, a Saturday, I lugged every cleaning utensil and every scouring powder in the house up to the hall where the bedrooms were. I laced into it. By the afternoon I had the hall and the first bedroom reasonably habitable.

'You're making great strides there,' said Mrs Houlihan, when she brought me some tea. 'Fit for a queen it is.'

I stood back and admired my work. 'Fit for a paying boarder, at least,' I admitted. If you stood still, you could hear the distant chug of the diesel engines. 'Any news about the guest coming?'

'It's all in progress. He won't be long in arriving.'

I got on with cleaning the bedrooms and going to school, spacing my rounds of Disturbance, and visiting Father Mulcahy desultorily. It was enough.

One day at school, Father Mooney came to deliver a talk. He was the parish priest who used sometimes take early Mass when Father Mulcahy had been out drinking the night before. I'd gathered he had it in for Father Mulcahy. I didn't know why.

The subject of the talk was 'The Temple of the Holy Ghost'. The term meant nothing to me. Father Mooney embarked in a low voice. The sun beamed through the window. I could feel a migraine coming on. I daydreamed.

I woke up. The priest was snapping his cane on the blackboard. On the blackboard he'd chalked the reference '1 Cor VI 19'. His cane snapped violently on this reference, while in a low trembling voice that belied the conviction of his cane, he said, 'Your body is the Temple of the Holy Ghost.'

I wondered was he confused. His gaze was fixed on the corner of the classroom, as if only the poster of Wild Flowers in Danger remained to be convinced. All I could sense from the class was a desperate silence. The sun through the panes bore on my head. Curiously, I felt I wanted to say something. I wanted to help the poor confused priest and shout at the recalcitrant poster, 'Yes! It really is true! Your body really is the Temple of the Holy Ghost!'

The notion was ridiculous. I sniggered. A chalk grazed my left ear. 'Shut up your filthy mind,' said Father Mooney. I had a feeling then that the talk might be about sex. Some seniors had nudged us that one was due. But I wasn't sure.

Because I wore glasses I sat at the front of the class. I could see the pulse in the priest's temple banging in and out. He breathed very quickly. His pulse slowly calmed. 'Well,' he said. 'Your parents will have mentioned the subject to you.'

It was a question.

Nobody answered.

'Well,' he said again, still addressing the poster of Wild Flowers in Danger. He crushed a chalk slowly in his fingers. The dust floated through a sunbeam to the floor. Then he swiped his hands on his soutane.

'We'll keep it anonymous so, lads.'

He had spoken to us directly at last. He took out from his case a wad of paper and distributed strips of it around the class. 'You needn't sign the paper at all, lads.' He was on our side now. His voice was friendly, avuncular. 'Just write down if you know about it, and who told you if you do.'

Hiding my mouth in the folds of my sleeve, I whispered to the boy next to me. 'What are you writing?'

He shrugged. 'I don't know. My parents.'

'Is this it?' I asked.

'What?'

'The sex talk?'

He shrugged. 'Is it?'

A chalk grazed my right ear. 'Shut up your dirty whispering,' said the priest. 'I have my eye on you.'

I could not recollect either my mother or my father mentioning anything about temples to me, but I remembered some time before Father Mulcahy had shown me some sketches he had made of churches. I wondered had the Temple of the Holy Ghost been amongst them. It seemed a peculiar test for a parish priest to set, but I had been upbraided often enough for daydreaming. Perhaps I'd missed something earlier.

Father Mooney instructed us to fold the papers twice over. Then he toured the aisles, his glance avoiding ours, as we dropped our replies into his hat. It was a curious business. I was reminded of a Mass I'd attended in the country where the collector seemed so ashamed when a coin rattled in the plate instead of a silent note that he pretended not to see the culprit. Once more I had the suspicion that somewhere within this talk must lurk 'sex'. But the Holy Ghost, though I had no clear notion of His function, could surely have nothing to do with that business.

The priest sat down at the table in front and opened and read to himself each reply in turn. The more he read, the more relaxed he became. We waited in silence.

'I'm glad to see from these replies,' he said half-way through, 'that your parents have been living up to the responsibilities of a Catholic family.' He coughed. 'Makes the task in hand a good deal less awkward.' He coughed again. 'For all of us. Well done, lads.' And it seemed he truly was glad. The red temper departed his face.

It was only when he came to my reply that all hell broke loose.

When eventually they'd finished with me, I ran home and ran straight up to my bedroom. I wedged the door shut with the torn fold in the carpet, the way it would look like the door had got wedged by mistake, in case anyone came knocking. I tore off every stitch of clothing I had on.

I stared at myself in the full-length mirror that hung inside the door to my wardrobe. But I could discern no noticeable difference – neither from what I had looked like yesterday nor from the other boys at school. Everything was there and in reasonable working order.

And yet, apparently, I had been interfered with. I didn't know whether to be pleased or shocked.

I dressed in my Saturday clothes and blindly swiped a slab from my jigsaw. It took me three hours to put it right again. In my perplexity I'd disrupted nearly a whole sixteenth of the surface.

Later, I told my father about what had happened at school. But he didn't take it very seriously. I could tell. Certainly, it didn't move him.

I didn't bother with school the next day. I had no stomach for any more inquisitions. I stayed in my bedroom and watched the workmen down the street. They were slower at their work than at first I had imagined. Slow, but very precise. It wasn't all chaotic like a disturbed ant's nest. Or the way I played Disturbance. They carried out their task thoroughly, demolishing one thing at a time. It was horrible to watch, and yet fascinating. I'd never thought breakers and wreckers would be so organized. It didn't sound right.

And yet you had to admire them. If I was a breaker or a wrecker, that's certainly the way I'd have gone about it.

The workmen stopped at five. I had nothing to do then. At five-thirty I decided it was time to visit Father Mulcahy.

He wasn't there.

'He's gone away,' the housekeeper snarled at me. 'And you, you filthy vermin, you've no business coming here no more.'

'Who is it?' called a voice inside. It was Father Mooney, the parish priest. He came to the door.

'You,' he said. I turned away. I'd had enough of his interrogating me, yesterday. 'Father Mulcahy's been sent away. He won't be back.'

I decided I hated the parish priest. For a man in his position he had an altogether vulgar accent. As I wandered off, I saw the blind begging piano accordionist on the steps of the church. It occurred to me he had nowhere to stay. It occurred to me Father Mulcahy would have nowhere to stay. So what, I thought.

When I got home, I heard a scurrying about above in the bedroom I'd recently cleaned out. So! The guest had finally arrived! Mrs Houlihan had worked her magic. I peeped round the door. It was Father Mulcahy.

I was about to say something – something very, very nasty – but I stopped, gaped. It was Father Mulcahy, all right, but suddenly he looked very small. It took a moment for me to understand. He wasn't wearing his black clerical suit. He was wearing a sports jacket. And his jacket was new, unworn, cheap. He had the look of a man selling utensils, door-to-door. He hadn't seen me. I crept away.

There was nothing for it but to confront my father.

But he just laughed at me. He actually laughed.

I stamped my foot. 'But that man has interfered with me! I told you last night! And you think that's funny?'

'But it was your idea, Nilus.'

'What was my idea?'

'You told me the parish priest was trying to get rid of him. You said he'd have nowhere to stay.'

'I said no such thing.'

My father studied me, quizzically. 'You really don't remember, do you?'

'Of course I don't remember! How could I remember? I didn't say it! This is one of your jokes, isn't it?'

My father sighed. Then the real truth came out. 'Anyway,' he said. 'I took pity on him.'

'Pity? What about me?'

He gnawed thoughtfully on a clove of garlic. 'Look at it this way, Nilus.' He started waving the remains of the garlic bulb about him, in a gesture of reasonableness, so that

72

the stench of his breath was wafted in my direction. 'He spends the greater part of his life mouthing off his Catholic rigmarole baloney, stuffing impressionable young heads with all manner of nonsense, warping minds left, right and centre. And all to great and public acclaim. Then all he has to do is touch one miserable sickly boy's body – not even touch it by all accounts – and suddenly he's out on his ear. Why wouldn't I take pity on him?'

I understood there was some sort of logic to what my father said, but it was a thin logic, the same thinness that permeated his laughter. I watched him. He was pouring himself a tumbler of brandy. He seemed really to be enjoying himself. It was near impossible to get any real sense out of him at all. There was no way of telling, but I wondered how long would this mania for jokey and sideways behaviour endure.

'My body isn't miserable,' I said. 'Nor sickly.'

'There you are then. What did I tell you? He hasn't done you any harm at all.' He saluted me with his tumbler. 'Cheers now,' he said.

At the dinner table that evening, in the big dining-room, Father Mulcahy joined us. He sneaked into the room. He was wearing an open-necked shirt, like a door-to-door salesman off duty.

'Okey-dokey,' said Mrs Houlihan, 'sit you where you will. We won't stand on ceremony here.'

He sat beside me. He nodded to his place mat. 'Nilus,' he said in a diminutive greeting. I moved inches away.

Mrs Houlihan deposited her efforts on the table. The priest half-grabbed at his cutlery.

'What about grace?' I said.

'Grace?' repeated Father Mulcahy, then lanced an almost supplicatory look at Mrs Houlihan.

'Grace,' she said, giving her smile. 'If you'd any sense, Father, you'd have married her.'

My father wasn't there. He was still in his bed. But I knew if he had been there, he would be laughing with them. Laughing, joking, thinly as they.

I bumped into my aunt one day outside my school. Actually, I suppose, she must have been waiting for me. There was precious little reason otherwise for hanging about in our awful neighbourhood.

'Nilus,' she said.

'Hello – er –' I didn't know if she was still Nessie, or had reverted to Agnes. It was safest to say nothing. As soon as I'd worked this out, I grew worried she might think I'd forgotten who she was altogether. 'Hello Auntie,' I said quickly. 'Aunt,' I added, just in case.

'I hoped I'd find you, Nilus. Well, we both did. Your Uncle Frank is waiting in the café. What would you say to a cup of coffee? And a tasty? You'd like a tasty, I'm sure. What do you say?'

'Café,' I repeated doubtfully. 'I don't think you'll find any cafés around here. Not now.'

'What do you mean?' she said. 'There's one across the road. Your Uncle Frank's waiting for us there.'

I followed the direction of her nod, and true enough there was a café there. It even said so on the sign. 'Ronnie's Broadway Café', it said. Then beneath a representation in thin neon of bubbles and a straw in a cocktail saucer, was the caption, 'Teas, Coffees, Snacks'.

I was dumbfounded. Why had I never noticed it before? It was outlandish. Somehow, I had neglected to remember there might still be shops operating in our neighbourhood. But when I looked, squinting, I saw there were still quite a few concerns going. 'Olympic Records', said a music shop. 'Wavelengths', said a hairdresser's. 'All She Wants', said a shop that appeared to be selling women's clothing. In fact, the street was chock-a-block with shops. There were people milling about. The place had an air of business about it.

I began to wonder did I really daydream my time away, mooching about with my eyes seeing no further than the cracked lines on the pavement below me, worrying my way to the next round of Disturbance.

'He didn't want to wait outside the school,' my aunt was saying as we crossed the road, 'in case your father came to collect you. I mean after that terrible message you relayed.'

I wanted to ask what message, but the traffic was too crazy, coming in all directions. It annoyed me that she was speaking, even. When we were finally safely across the road, I said, 'How can you talk while we're in the road? Don't you know you're supposed to watch and listen?'

She leaned her head to a pose of consideration. 'Well, yes,' she said. 'But the lights were green, Nilus.'

As if you could rely on electricity to see you safe.

'What message?' I asked as we entered the café.

'Why, the message your father sent. That if he caught Frankie talking to you, or interfering with you, as he put it, he'd have the guards on to him. You telephoned, remember?'

'Oh yes.' I remembered now.

'There you are,' said my uncle. He put away his paper. 'Pull up a chair, Nilus. Nessie, see if you can't get the boy some coffee.'

So she was still my Auntie Nessie.

'Would you like a tasty, Nilus?'

76

'All right.'

'You see, Nilus,' began my uncle, all business-like.

'Now, what sort of a tasty would you like?' said my aunt, butting in.

I twisted the corner of one end of my mouth. 'I don't know what sort they have.'

'I'm sure they have all sorts. Barn-brack with butter? Frankie used to so love his barn-brack with butter when he was your age. Well, actually, I suppose, he was older than you.' She tilted her head confidentially towards me. 'I didn't know your uncle till he had achieved his majority.' She regained her upright posture. 'Barn-brack, so, with butter?'

'All right.'

'Lemon cheese topping, or jam?'

'Look, just fetch the boy a coffee,' said my uncle, losing his patience.

'Well, Frankie, I did promise him a tasty.'

'Well, get him a tasty, then.'

'But he hasn't told me which topping he prefers.'

'I just don't see why you have to make all this fuss about it.'

'I don't want to get him a tasty he won't eat. I keep thinking of the poor Africans. Or is it the Asians?'

He turned on me now. 'Nilus: tell your aunt which tasty you want.'

'Lemon cheese topping, or jam,' my aunt reminded me.

I had never had barn-brack before, with or without butter. Squinting at the shelf on the far counter, I could make out a tray of choice Danish pastries – my favourites at the time. But I could tell it would be really asking for it even to mention a personal preference. I sighed.

'Lemon cheese,' I said.

77

'Very well.' She took out her purse.

I hoped to get this over with soon. I wanted to go home. Although, of course, it was too early actually to play Disturbance, I liked to check on my jigsaw after school. After all, I'd been without it since morning.

'Right,' said my uncle. 'Let's get down to business. I've brought the plans with me, Nilus. I thought you might like a quick look-see.'

'Frankie,' said my Auntie Nessie.

'What is it now?'

'I just wondered if you might want a tasty?'

'No I don't.'

'Well, there's no need to shout. I'm doing my best.'

'Yes, Nessie. You're certainly doing your best.'

There was a shambling at the door, and the blind beggarman piano accordionist shuffled in. He left his battered unpleasant case by the door, tapped his way with his stick to a table, tapped around the floor underneath to make sure no one was sitting there, deposited his hat on one chair. Then he went back to the door to fetch his case.

'And these plans, Nilus,' my uncle was saying, 'they've all been approved. God knows, we might be in for an award with this one.'

'An award,' I repeated. 'Yes.'

I'd gazed at his plans for what I'd judged a suitable length of time. They meant nothing to me. The blind beggarman on the table in front was staring out into space, with a somewhat surprised look on his face. Suddenly, he reached into his pocket, found something, felt around its edges, shook it in his hand, then replaced it in his pocket. 'All jigs and reels,' he muttered, sadly to himself.

'So really,' said my uncle, 'there's no cause for this

carry-on of your father's. No cause at all. The way to look on it is as an improvement.'

'An improvement,' I said.

'Well, except –'

'Except what, Nessie?'

'Except . . .' She pondered, double-checking what she was going to say. She apparently found it still reasonable. 'Except he doesn't want to have to move house.'

'How can you say that, Nessie? I've just convinced the boy it's a good move. And now you have to interfere with your useless tuppence-worth.'

'But it's the truth, Frankie. Your brother doesn't want to move.'

'Nessie, I'm talking business here. Truth?' He swept his hands back briskly behind his head, in a gesture, I presumed, of exasperation. Actually, it came out like he was trying to brush some uncommon restraint from his shoulders. 'Anyway, it's not his decision. That old shambles is mine now. By rights. Along with the cottages. I have the deeds.'

'Well, of course I know that, Frankie. What I'm saying is, your brother doesn't want to give up the family home. That's all. It's quite understandable, really.'

My uncle looked at my aunt, looked at me, looked at the piano accordionist at the table in front of us. 'Look Nessie, you know as much about this subject as that blind man there. Now, just keep out of it.'

'Very well. If that's the way you feel.'

'That's the way I feel.'

'Very well.'

There was an awkward silence for a moment. Then my aunt said, in her ever so reasonable voice, 'Except, Frankie, I think I know a *little* bit more than the blind man does.'

'Oh God,' said my uncle. 'Nilus, what do you say?'

I could see he was going to start on me now. 'I don't know,' I said – I thought, safely.

'I don't know what's wrong with you, Nilus. You always say "I don't know." Don't you have an opinion?'

'My father won't have anything to do with it, that's all.' Oh God, I prayed, get me out of this.

'Well, he's got two more months to have nothing to do with it. Then he's out on his ear. I won't have any more of this carry-on. I'm a patient man, Nilus. But enough is enough. Is he still sending you to the bank every Monday to collect his cheque?'

'Yes.'

'Well, that'll end too. Unless we get some sense out of him.'

He stood up. 'Come on, Nessie, it's time we were away.'

'But, Frankie, we haven't touched on that other subject.'

'What other subject?'

'You remember: Ira and – and her beau.'

'You think I want to squander my time on that joker?'

'But you promised. You said we'd talk to Nilus. Nilus is here now. Let's talk to him. Come on, Frankie. You did promise. Then we'll go home and I'll cook a nice meal. One of your favourites.'

My uncle sat down heavily. 'Okay, okay, I know when I'm beaten. You talk to him.'

My aunt leaned over the table closer to me. 'Well, Nilus, it's like this.' She paused. 'Would you like some more coffee? Another tasty, perhaps?'

I counted the sachets of sugar in the bowl. There were five white and eight brown. I calculated the dimensions of the sachets, and reckoned they were rectangles whose sides were exactly twice the length of their top and bottom ends. This pleased me. I discounted the five whites, however. Odd numbers were always difficult to do anything at all regular with. But it occurred to me, if I concentrated only on the eight sachets of brown sugar, then I might soon have a decent square on the table in front of me. I still had to put up with Auntie Nessie bleating on, though.

'The thing is,' she was saying, either to me or to my uncle, I wasn't sure, 'Ira's left her apartment and moved back home. And that beau of hers, well he couldn't possibly afford to stay on in that apartment by himself. Not without Ira's allowance. So of course, he doesn't really have anywhere to live now.'

'He could try getting a job,' my uncle cut in.

My aunt chewed this over. She took a sachet of white sugar, tore it open, and left it to pour out slowly into her coffee. By this time, I had seven of the brown sachets already laid out in front of me. I was just contemplating the eighth and final rectangle that would complete my perfect square, when my aunt, right before my eyes, reached into the bowl and stole it.

I couldn't believe it. I watched stupefied as the brown grains spilled out into her coffee, filtering down as interminably slowly as sand in an egg-timer. She stirred the concoction distractedly with her spoon, an innocuous expression on her face. But nobody had white sugar *and* brown. Nobody. What did my aunt think she was at?

I gazed at the glaring imperfection of my square. For a moment I nearly panicked. I had no idea what to do.

'Yes, he *could* get a job,' she conceded eventually to my uncle. It was beyond belief; she was *still* rattling on about the joker. 'But he seems to think if he did that he'd be some sort of racing capitalist dog. Greyhound, I suppose.'

'Look,' said my uncle, 'if you're going to use those terms, at least get them right: a running dog of capitalism.'

She considered this. 'Sugar, Nilus?'

'No,' I managed to murmur. She had screwed up her empty sachet, but she still kept it in her hand. There was nothing for it but to wait for her to dispose of it. And in the meantime endure an imperfect square dead in front of me.

'The thing is, it's such a shame. He's young now –'

'Young?' Uncle Frank butted in again. 'He's a bloody imbecile.'

'Well, of course he's young, Frankie. They're both young. He might be a little wild now –'

'Wild? He's a bloody maniac.'

She looked at her hand, seemed to wonder what the screwed-up sachet could be doing there, dropped it into the ashtray. 'But he'll grow out of it,' she said.

I snatched it up and began a desperate smoothing operation on my lap.

'Grow out of it? That joker? I'll believe that when I see it.'

'Well, you grew out of it, Frankie.'

'Me? What d'you mean by that?'

'Don't you remember? Oh, it was so funny. When I first met you. You were always ranting and raving about something or other. Oh, it did so make me laugh.'

He started in his chair. I glanced up at him. 'You laughed, Nessie?' He looked all stung. Like she'd played a dirty trick. Like he was a dog and she'd pinched his long-buried bone. Or he was me, and she'd stolen the final component of his square. 'Nessie, you *laughed*? Those were my principles you were laughing at.'

'Well, it was a funny set of principles. Never washing, never working, never going to church, never paying rent.'

'But, Nessie, I was a socialist. I didn't believe in those

things, I didn't have time for those things. I was trying to save the world, for God's sake.'

'That doesn't mean you have to smell.'

'So now you're saying I was smelly?'

'Well, of course you were smelly. A bit. Anybody smells who doesn't wash. It stands to reason.'

'Nilus: you tell her. You're a young man.'

'Tell her what?'

'Tell her there are more important things than smelling sweet. When you're young, I mean.'

I should've known he'd pick on me eventually. I just nodded. In truth, I couldn't understand why these people had to talk like this. It was so unnecessary, disordered. As if I didn't have enough problems with brainchill and my jigsaw and getting the boarding-house sorted out. As if my father hadn't gone and turned sideways in his behaviour. As if the used sachet hadn't blasted for ever the conception of my square. As if –

My uncle shook his head. 'I don't know, Nilus . . . Anyway,' he returned to my aunt, '*I* got off my backside, found myself a job.'

'Well, that's not exactly true, either. When you asked me to marry you, I told you then what you must do. Full marks, you did it. You apologized to your poor father, and asked him could you try your hand at the family business. And what a success you made of it! Then you branched out into construction. It was the making of you. And I told you then, if you want to be a socialist or whatever it was, you can vote Labour. So everybody was happy.'

My uncle threw a sardonic face in my direction. I tried to echo it, but it probably came out a pasty simper. I was far too preoccupied imagining the seven remaining sachets into some acceptably regular shape. A heptagon, I thought. But how to describe a heptagon?

My aunt was carping on regardless. I felt I should at least pretend to listen. 'Ira and – and her beau, they haven't given each other a chance yet. And a home without a father is not the place for a child to grow up.' She thought a minute. 'Grow up in,' she corrected herself. 'Her baby's due soon. Won't be long now. And I'm just worried.'

'Look, Nessie. You talk to Nilus if you want to. I'll wait in the car. I haven't got all day.'

He left. He didn't even say goodbye. Just banged into the blind piano accordionist's case as he passed. My aunt continued. She was talking about something or other.

The blind beggarman stood up. I watched him; there was sugar on his table. He yawned slightly, stretched a bit. 'All jigs and reels,' he said. 'You wouldn't get the price of a cup of tea, but they're wanting jigs and reels off of you.' He was fussing with his accordion case, talking to himself. 'I lost my eyes in the service of Ireland, but 'tis all jigs and reels since.' He had telescoped his blind man's stick to fit in his pocket. Now he took it out, expanded it again. 'Jigs and reels. Nothing but jigs and reels.'

He shuffled off.

As soon as he was away. I shot my hand over to his table, snatched a sachet of brown sugar from the bowl there, and collapsed back into my chair. I had the makings of a real square at last.

My aunt hadn't even noticed. She seemed to be getting ready herself to leave.

'I knew I could rely on you, Nilus,' she was saying. 'Of course it's only for a short time. Naturally. None of you will be there for long now. But if he could just stay in the bosom of the family, there might still be a chance. Of reconciliation.'

The peculiar thing was that, as soon as I had positioned

the eighth sachet on the table in front of me, perfecting my square, a longing burned into my head to remove it again. I couldn't quite work it out. It seemed a madness. Then it hit me. It was five-thirty in the evening. Time for Disturbance.

I grabbed at the eighth sachet, counted ten, then carefully replaced it in the square.

It was Disturbance, all right.

I felt nearly happy, and I actually smiled. My aunt thought I was smiling at her.

'Thank you, Nilus,' she said. 'I would have approached your father myself, but the way things stand between Frankie and him, I do feel rather awkward.'

I perked up at this. She was apparently talking about my father. '*You* feel awkward,' I said. 'What about me? I don't know when he's serious and when he's joking any more. And he comes out with the weirdest ideas. I mean, yesterday he wanted to know why I wear my glasses all the time. I mean to say.'

'Yes,' she said, musing. 'I must admit I've often wondered that.'

'What d'you mean?'

'Well, you're long-sighted, aren't you? You only really need your glasses for reading. But you do seem to wear them rather a lot.'

'My mother told me I had to wear my glasses.'

'All the time?'

'Look,' I said, 'I have to leave.' I grabbed at the sachet again, counted ten, then replaced it. But the novelty had worn off. It wasn't really Disturbance, after all. It was a fraud.

I had one last go at explaining. 'Don't you see, Auntie Nessie? It's so *disordered*. I'm frightened my father is joking and being serious at the same time. It's just *disordered*.'

85

It was clear the silly woman had no idea what I was talking about. No idea of the gravity of the situation.

All she said was, 'Well, perhaps things will be better when Ira's beau moves in. You'll have someone to talk to then.'

I left her to it. I hesitated a moment outside, looking to see if the blind beggarman piano accordionist was still about. I didn't know why. My mother used to play the piano accordion. We still had her old instrument at home. Somewhere.

It was way past time I played Disturbance. I hurried off home.

Ira's beau moving in, I pondered as I trudged through the colourless streets. What was the silly woman on about now?

And of course, the joker, Ira's beau, Joe Maloney, whatever; he did come to stay. But he wasn't the very next guest. I came home one evening and the blind piano accordionist was perched at the kitchen table.

I swerved and was back-tracking out, quiet as a mouse, but he still heard me.

'Is that young Niall Moore?'

I paid no attention, but sought out Mrs Houlihan.

'What's that blind man doing in the kitchen?'

'John Mitchell? You remember John Mitchell, don't you? Used to live down the street –'

'I know where he used to live. What's he doing in the kitchen?'

'Poor lamb, he's come to stay, sure.'

'Mrs Houlihan, what sort of boarding-house are we running here? We have nothing but child molesters and blind beggars. I can't see this impressing my uncle.'

'Who wants to impress your uncle?'

'I do, of course.'

She was dusting away in one of the spare bedrooms. It seemed absurd to me. I'd never seen anyone dust rubble before.

'Poor lamb, are you here to lend a hand?'

'A hand doing what?'

'Why, we could move some of this stuff out of the way. We don't want John Mitchell tripping over the furniture, do we?'

Furniture, she called it. 'Rubble,' I corrected her.

'Head over heels,' she continued, heedless, 'tripping lock, stock and barrel, he will be.'

I supposed it was a reasonable enough request. And so, while I informed her of the class of boarder we really wanted to attract, I helped her clean out and tidy up the bedroom for the blind beggar.

She clapped her hands. 'Okey-dokey,' she said. 'That's done. Cup of tea suit you?'

I shambled after her down the stairs. Somehow or other, I thought, I never got to the point where people actually attended to what I was saying.

'You're keeping well, John Mitchell,' she said as she charged the kettle.

'I'm all right, Missus. Though 'twas desperate straits of late.'

'It was in the cards, John Mitchell. It was in the cards. But you're here now.'

'I am that.'

Because he was blind, I was able to stare at him, study him reasonably closely. He had two false eyes. They'd obviously been positioned by some wandering quack. They were fixed staring upwards and to the right, giving him a look of continuous surprise or puzzlement. He had an appalling mouth. It was wet and all over the place. His blind man's stick was rusty and greyed, and he banged it on the floor about him even when he was sat still. His old battered accordion case was beside him. Though I could detect no particular smell, neither sweet nor noisome, I was undecided whether to call him a tramp or not. There was a hole beginning in one of his boots.

Mrs Houlihan delivered his tea. He made a great play of fumbling his hand along the table edge, over the saucer-top to circle the lip of the cup. 'I'll need a feel around before I'm at home, Missus.'

'You'll be right as rain.'

'Shouldn't be allowed,' he said, as if continuing the same conversation. 'Them cottages was homes. They'd stand a century or more. Left standing.'

'I've stirred your tea,' said Mrs Houlihan.

I went to speak to my father.

'Paeans,' he said from between his pillows.

'Paeans?' I asked.

'You come in here chattering away your paeans.'

'Paeans?' I said again.

'Look it up.'

'Dad,' I said, 'why won't you tell me a story? Like you used.'

He reached for his brandy bottle. 'Like I used?'

'Yes.'

'Sure, I never told you any stories.'

'But you did.'

'Get away out of that. It was you were the storyteller. Always going on about some tale or other. Delaying your sleep, I called it. And all your hedge priests and your blind bards and your beautiful Mother Erins – sure you were

88

always making up some story or other. *I* used have to sit and listen to them. A right pain in the arse they were, too.'

Later, after dinner, when we were all sat by the fire – I mean everybody but my father, who remained in his bed – John Mitchell said to me, 'What tune would you like me to play, young Niall?'

'Why d'you keep calling me Niall?'

'Isn't that your name?'

'My name's Nilus.'

'That's a strange name for a young Irish man.'

Was it? I'd never thought about it before. 'Play anything you like.'

'The old tunes are the best,' said Mrs Houlihan.

'Like the jokes,' added Father Mulcahy, then he looked anxiously up at Mrs Houlihan as if to ascertain was it all right him speaking.

Something had come over Father Mulcahy since he'd wormed his way into my home. It was difficult to pinpoint what exactly. His voice was losing its chest register, but not only the timbre had changed; it was like the nerve, too, had gone. He looked a pitiable specimen, done up in his cheap jacket, a handout, no doubt, from the Vincent de Paul. But worst of all were his eyes, and the way they had to glance to Mrs Houlihan the whole time, always seeking her approval. Maybe that was it. He just wasn't confident enough, any more, to be nasty.

It was like coming home from safari with a toothless circus lion.

John Mitchell embarked on some tune or other. It sounded remotely familiar. 'Believe Me, If All those Endearing Young Charms', I think. There was an oompah-oompah bass over a thin keyboard. The bellows jerked between his arms and his foot thumped out the rhythm. His own expression didn't change at all while he played, but Mrs Houlihan smiled sweetly and Father Mulcahy forgot about his cigarette so that the ash grew down to his fingers undisturbed.

'I could teach you a chord or two if you liked, young Niall,' he said afterwards. Because he was blind I didn't contradict him again about my name. He looked surprisedly above me and to my right. 'I used teach the piano accordion.'

'Before you went blind?'

'Not at all. Before it was all jigs and reels. I'll teach you for free too, I will. One good turn deserves another. Isn't that so? One good turn deserves another.'

'What d'you mean?'

'And wasn't it you told me about the boarding-house?'

Yes, I suppose I had told him about the boarding-house. But how could I have known he was going to move in?

I believe I cried in the middle of the night. John Mitchell was playing 'Nobody's Child' over and over again in some distant part of the house. It had unpleasant chords. It was the song my mother had always made me sing when we had visitors at Christmas.

M ostly, the bulldozers just droned away in the distance. But for a time, when they were razing the cottages directly opposite, they sounded inordinately close. All that week, no matter where I went or what I did, I had the rumour of them in my ear.

They had most of the cottages on the left-hand side of the street, the side opposite to us, flattened now. Soon they would start on our side.

From the gable window, high up in my garret, I watched a cottage come down. I found it fascinating how they went about it. They got a crane with a ball swinging from it, and banged the ball against a wall till the wall gave way. The cottages never put up much of a resistance. So much for John Mitchell's opinion that they'd stand a century or more. Jerry-built, I said to myself. It never took long. And there was a satisfying rhythm to the way the ball swung. Like a game, almost.

I remembered the uncouth tradesmen-like children who used to play handball against those walls – in between the times they'd be vandalizing somebody else's property. My mother was always hot on to their vandalism. She was always knocking on someone's door complaining. Those children would almost certainly approve of this adult version of their game. I wondered where they'd all gone.

Good riddance. They used to annoy me with their loud

ways. They even used to find my school uniform funny. I'd no idea why. It was the most serious thing I owned. Before the jigsaw.

After the working men left for home, I wandered down the half-flattened street and sat down on the floor of an ex-cottage. Already grass was growing through cracks in the concrete base. There was nothing of interest. Just dull leftover bits of somebody else's life. I tugged on some grass. Then I saw myself being a vandal, and started to replant the clumps I'd pulled.

It was too quiet after the bulldozers' droning the day long. I couldn't think of anything to do. I wondered should I visit my father. Did he know I'd stopped going to school? What would he say if he knew? It was an interesting speculation. He might even be annoyed.

I stood up with a conviction and strode off to my father's bedroom.

Except I ended up knocking on Father Mulcahy's door.

'Who is it?' he called.

'Me,' I said. Then in case he'd forgotten, 'Nilus.'

'Oh.' He didn't open the door. 'What d'you want?'

'I wondered did you want to do my portrait?'

'What's that?'

'Look, can't I come in?'

He unlocked the door, opened it. 'Not now.'

But I stepped in anyway.

On the table near his window he had the cards laid out for patience. That's all he did these days: play patience. He sat down and, after an aeon's concentration, he placed a red queen beneath a red king. I was about to point out his error, but I stopped myself. It was just so tiresomely typical of him now that he couldn't even play cards properly.

'What d'you want knocking on my door?' he said eventually.

'Why won't you do my portrait?'

He looked around him. 'I've no pens here.'

'Pens?' That was a poor excuse. I sat down on his bed facing him, then took off my glasses. 'I just want to talk to someone.'

'What about?'

'Anything,' I said. I shrugged my hands. 'Evil thoughts. Anything.'

He let out a big long sigh, like all the world was contained in it. 'Evil thoughts,' he said. 'Evil thoughts,' he repeated.

I had a feeling for a moment that I was living in a whirlwind of treachery. Everything and everybody were changing, and right before my eyes. The street was disappearing, the house was falling down. Mrs Houlihan seemed hellbent on becoming a gypsy. Father Mulcahy grew meeker by the minute, docile as a paschal lamb. And my father was growing more and more contrary, like a black sheep in the fold. I had a feeling that everything was out of control, or that I had no control over anything any more.

Father Mulcahy looked so resigned. I was sick of him, sick of his room. 'Why did you have to change?' I said.

'Change, is it? You think you can keep a man, port him home with you, hold him to yourself, visit him when you're bored, and think you're keeping time still? All you're keeping is pickles in a jar. Pickles in a jar is all.'

In his voice he'd regained a scraping of the gravel and cinders of old. I was half-mollified by that. 'Why you couldn't just do my portrait while you were saying that, I don't know,' I remarked as I left.

I considered asking John Mitchell for my first piano accordion lesson. But the whole idea sounded far too energetic, taxing. I went to speak to my father.

'I've stopped going to school,' I announced.

But he wasn't annoyed. I suppose I should've known. Father Mulcahy had been meek; of course my father would be correspondingly contrary.

'Have you got your three Rs?' he asked.

'My three Rs?'

'Reading, writing and 'rithmetic.'

'Of course I have.'

'That's all right then.'

'What's all right?'

'So long as you have your Rs. In later life, you'll find it's always handy to have your *arse* to fall back on.'

I huffed. His joking and his drinking and his chewing garlic were bad enough, but now it appeared he was going to start using dirty language.

'Don't get so het up, Nilus. You've a face would boil red cabbage. It's only a jape.'

'So you don't mind if I don't go to school?'

'Let's face it, Nilus, you were never very academic-minded.'

'That's nonsense. I love school.'

'So? Why have you stopped going?'

He had me there. I didn't know what to say. He'd done it on purpose. He'd tricked me.

'You know yourself, Nilus. You don't love school. You just get carried away with things. Remember the Italian? You decided to take Italian classes, and you pestered me to buy all the books. Then you pestered me to learn it myself, so you'd have someone to converse with. Do you bother now? No. The books are still there. Do you open them? Nine-day wonder, everything is to you.'

He poured himself half a tumbler of brandy. 'You want a drink?'

'A drink?'

'Yes.'

'Me?'

'Yes, Nilus.'

'I don't believe this. You're offering me drink.'

'If you don't want one, just say so.' He watched me a moment, then tutted, sighed, emptied the brandy bottle into his glass.

I began roaming around the bedroom. 'I don't know where I am any more,' I was saying. 'There's you contradicting me left, right and centre. And what with Mrs Houlihan giving house space to child molesters and blind beggarmen, and Father Mulcahy pushing cigarettes on me day and night – I don't know where I am any more. Everything's changing. And now you're trying to turn me into an alcoholic. I'm supposed to be your son.'

'I'm only offering you a drink, Nilus. For God's sake. You're sixteen years old.'

'I'm not sixteen.'

'You *are* sixteen. Why don't you face it?' You seem to think time stopped when your mother died. You are sixteen years of age.'

I was angry. I was in a white hot temper. I stared fiercely at my black jigsaw puzzle. The bastard.

A thought embered into my mind that I might play Disturbance. But no way. My fingers were gripped too rigorously together. There was no way I could manage the intricate repositioning of the pieces. If I tore a corner away I might never get it back together again. And then where would I be?

All I could do was stare at the midnight black surface, impotently.

I cursed my father. Why was he always so – so *un-*

95

reasonable? So *unreliable*? Didn't he know that all I ever wanted was to be told?

Told what?

Just told.

Nobody seemed to care what I did. I stopped washing. I didn't know why. I stopped making my bed. My sheet-folds descended to a state of welter and peccancy. I stopped cleaning my room. I lay on the dishevelment of my bed and watched the dust gather on the cornice, on the rail on the dado. Enough dust, and they'd take on the look of a wave on the sea, never getting closer, just wilder with spume.

I had migraine. I was sure.

I knew it was important to think of nothing new. So in the morning I dressed in the clothes nearest to hand. This meant my school uniform. It would become unspeakably shabby with the ceaseless wear. But what was I to do?

I lay on my bed, all agony laden, with my dirty smell engulfing me. I could smell it everywhere. Anything I touched lingered with my smell. Nothing energetic; just staleness.

I said to Mrs Houlihan, when she brought me my supper tray, 'It's no use. I can't eat.'

'Poor lamb, you're off your food, is it?'

'And I'm sorry about the smell. I just hope you'll understand.'

'Smell?'

'It's probably my shirt. My vest. My underpants.' I was so helplessly resigned I could even mention underclothes to this relative stranger.

'What's wrong with your shirt?'

'It's just, Mrs Houlihan –' I waved my hand. The movement began as a categorical slice, but ended a despairing

96

limp through the air – 'I don't have the strength to change out of it.'

'Nilus,' she said, 'sure, didn't I launder that shirt the day before yesterday?'

'I know,' I agreed. I was shocked myself at my degeneration. Two days running in the same shirt. 'And I don't have the – I don't know – the *purpose* to change it. I'm just wearing the same clothes every day.'

'Since Tuesday?'

'Yes. I don't know what's happening to me.'

She started going on about something. She was saying it's only Thursday today or something. As if lassitude required a decade to show.

'Mrs Houlihan! I'm sick. Can't you see? I'm lying on sheets with imperfect folds. There's dust on my jigsaw. I keep thinking of words like "brainchill". And they don't exist. Look!' I grabbed for my dictionary so violently that the lamp by my bed clattered to the floor. 'Look it up. Brainchill. It's not there.'

'Poor lamb,' she said. 'And you say you're sick?'

'Of course I'm sick. I've been telling you. I didn't even change my underpants yesterday. Or today.'

'You young fellas, sure you're all alike. Leave them out tomorrow and I'll see to them.'

I closed my eyes. She was still there smiling when I opened them again. It occurred to me her smile had the staying power of a mountain.

'Mrs Houlihan,' I said quite calmly, 'my father doesn't take me seriously.'

'Poor lamb.' She tut-tutted. 'He's a lot on his mind, these days, you poor Da has.'

I chewed this over. He sure as hell should have. He had my death planned in the letters, my mother's death executed. He had this third stroke to look forward to. Even Atlas would baulk at the weight on his mind. I arched my eyebrows. 'Sins?' I hinted.

'Since the bulldozers, of course.'

'Mrs Houlihan –'

She was leaving. 'If you're sick, poor lamb, why don't you stay home tomorrow? No harm skipping school one day. Stay at home, why don't you?'

She didn't even know I'd stopped school. She didn't even care. Nobody cared.

I was getting sick of my own company. I went down for breakfast the next morning.

'Okey-dokey,' said Mrs Houlihan. 'You've taken my advice. A day off school and you'll be right as rain. You're mending splendid already. You'll see. Everything'll turn out hunky-dory. Like everything else.'

'Pass the milk,' I said.

While she was passing the milk, she had a fit of trembling. 'Oh dear,' she said. 'Oh dear.'

'Is it my mother?' I asked fretfully.

'Maureen? I don't know. So many voices, shouting poetry at me. So many voices.'

The fit passed. She mopped up the milk she had split.

'Nothing from my mother?'

'Poor lamb,' she said. 'You're anxious for news. Well, there was something about sheets. I didn't catch the whole message. Something about folding them. And then all the voices, lonely like lights off the strand.'

I left my bowl of cornflakes and made straight for my room. I hardly even noticed the rubble on the way, or felt the cobwebs, or smelt the damp and garlic. I made my bed.

While I was doing this, I caught a flashing glimpse of

myself in my full-length mirror. I was dressed in my school uniform. No wonder I felt sick. Anyone would feel distressed doing that. The disorder of it. Inconsistency. Wearing a school uniform when you weren't going to school. No wonder I felt so sick. I leaped out of my uniform and into my Saturday clothes.

I felt better then, like a new man. Things were looking up. When I'd finished a furious spring-clean of my room, I thought about the other bedrooms. It seemed I was only truly happy when I was cleaning things. I could maybe make a start on the other rooms. Time would pass.

We had seven bedrooms in all. Four were occupied: my own, my father's, John Mitchell's and Father Mulcahy's. That still left three. I inspected them. They were a disgrace.

I was gratified. There was a mountain of work in them.

In the broom cupboard where I was searching out scouring powders and utensils, I caught a whiff of passing garlic. I went straight to my father in his bedroom.

'Why d'you never get up?' I demanded.

He chewed lazily on his bulb. 'Maybe I'm tired.'

'That's no excuse.'

'It wasn't tendered as an excuse. It's a reason.'

I was sorely tempted to use bad language.

'The spare rooms are a disgrace,' I said busily. 'They're knee-deep in rubble.'

'Nilus,' he said, 'why must you always make alps of knaps? Where anyone else would see a little dust that a hoovering might equal, you must fancy an advancing glacier of rubble. Whenever you talk, you always give the impression the next ice age approacheth. I'm getting worried about you, Nilus. Are you sick?'

I had no time – and was in no mood – for his perversities. I got on with the business at hand.

One night, I sat in the breakfast room by the fire, with the others. I had the big dictionary down. I was going through the Bs, from 'baa' (to bleat) to 'byword' (a proverbial example). I was searching for a word that might sound like 'brainchill'.

These days, after I'd got over my forty-eight hours of dirty protest, I felt more relaxed and calm. In the breakfast room, Mrs Houlihan would be reading her tarot cards or assisting Father Mulcahy at his patience. So relaxed was I that I could nearly forgive the man his unreasonable transformation. Sometimes, I even helped him myself. I was that calm. John Mitchell would play soft tunes on his accordion. There would be turf on the fire. I'd feel satisfied after my day's hard labour with the rubble removal from the bedrooms. I could relax with my feet on the fender.

The words in the dictionary started a straying dance before my eyes. The scent of the turf drifted from the fire. I closed my eyes. My mother had always burned coal. It was disloyal, I knew, but, compared to this, coal had a hard smell, like a sore throat. The scent from the turves faltered on the air, and I imagined a small cosy home with a lamp burning in the window, warm but in some way industrious with it, and all around the heather and the wind and the distant miles . . .

I had dozed off. I half-woke to a mellow voice talking, soft like rain in the country.

It was my father. He was finally telling me a story. I was so happy. And he had put on a voice that a storyteller would put on if he were telling to a child a *fadó fadó* – once upon a time – tale. It was such a homely voice, the sort you felt you could snuggle up into. It was the sort of voice that told you about old things that had passed, and you thought if only you could listen long and intently enough you'd regain something. Something you didn't even know you'd lost.

I half-dozed behind my eyelids, and snuggled up into my father's soft and slow and antique voice . . .

'The street was lined with mourners,' he was saying, 'and the shops were closed, and the fine linen of the curtains was drawn across the windows, but not against the wind, and the candles burned lowly on dampened sills. And the women in blackest black, and the men in darkest grey, and all in their Sunday best, all lined the street, with their faces lined and hanging drawn.'

Yes, I thought. Yes, I thought. I was so happy. My father was actually telling me a story. I could scarcely believe my ears. Nor did I dare open my eyes lest the twinkling of an eyelid should disturb him.

'And with slowness and care beyond precision, the slow mournful procession passed. And it passed between the two extremities of the road, between the women and the men, between the two extremities of this life, and the christening church behind it and the burial ground beyond – between the mourners and the mourners, and the quick shuffling of limbs as men blessed themselves and the soul of the so recently departed. And as the cortège wound its way along the ribbon of track to the hilleen above, all eyes turned to follow its wake, and viewed in turn the earth beneath them and the heavens above them and the body stiff between. And as they watched, the slow anguish of a keen was set up inside the carriage, now low, now piercing high, tender and soft and worshipful, as the three poor wretches of womanhood grieved their loss: the mother, the widow, the daughter so quickly fatherless.'

I had never visited the West, but I recognized this scene. I knew this village, this street. I knew the grey sky and the soft rain and the smell on the breath of these people. This place was home, as the grave of a grandfather is home.

My father continued. 'And out from the mourning men stepped the old Sean-an-tí, Niall Moore of the black hair was his name. And out to greet him manly stepped the blind bard and the hedge priest a-wandering. "Niall Moore of the black hair," said the blind bard and the hedge priest a-wandering, bearded with long wisdom, the both of them: "Is it not true that yonder wail is the saddest, most pitiful, melancholy wail you would hear or hope to hear on this grey earth after year upon year of tribulation and loss, and its sweet tenderness giving tongue to the pain and dulling the senses, and beautiful all in all?"'

'On the contrary,' my father said.

I was shocked awake. It was suddenly his normal voice. His normal sideways voice. I tried to open my eyes. They had moistened with something or other, tears. They were sticking, I couldn't open them.

'On the contrary,' my father repeated, and I could feel him leaning towards me, almost poking me with his glint, 'for old Mother Houlihan, the old Hag of Erin, had told him so: "On the contrary," said Niall Moore of the black, black hair, "it's a paean in the hearse," he said,' said my father.

My eyes catapulted open. I was shivering. The lights were out. The fire was in its embers. It was so quiet, the silence raged. I hated the dark. Everybody had gone to bed. There was nobody there.

When Joe Maloney came to stay I found myself talking to him in a Northern Irish accent. He wasn't from Northern Ireland himself, of course. He was a Dubliner, born and bred. From Finglas, presumably – or some such salt-of-the-earth neighbourhood. Anyway, he went on about the North the whole time. And to show him that I didn't dislike him inordinately and that, in fact, I pitied him rather, I took on the harsher twang of Ulster when we spoke together. It was, if you like, a voice of sympathy.

And he did go on about the North. I understood what a complicated problem it must be by the number of polysyllabic words required to speak about it.

'Know what I mean, Nilus, it's the oligarchy of them multinational industrialists, North, South and across the Water, that are pre-empting the unification of the proletariat, in their own interest – you with me? – to further the sectarian divide, and thereby attenuating and neutralizing – know what I mean? – the legitimate demands of wage labour.'

'Aye,' I said in my Northern Irish twang.

And he did seem comforted. 'I mean,' he went on, 'like, I really agree – I'm really in accordance – with your Da. It's an act of gross defiance, like. I mean, I'm one hundred per cent with him.'

'You agree with my father?' This was real nonsense. 'What's there to agree about with my father?'

'Exactly,' he replied, 'Precisely. Any thinking man wouldn't give it a second thought. This day and age, we have to know whose bread we're buttering. It's time for the barricades. Not like them traitorous bastards outside.'

'Who?'

'Traitors to their class. Bulldozing away. Them cottages was dwellings. Where d'they live now? Turfed out on the street, they were. To line a rich man's pocket. Connolly predicted as much. Marx too. What's that smell?' he asked suddenly.

'Oh, the smell,' I said. 'You may well ask.'

'Bit whiffy, isn't it?'

'Damn right it's whiffy – I mean, strong.' I didn't like using his vulgar phrases if I could help it. 'It's my father.'

He eyed me queerly, 'Your father?'

'Garlic,' I said, knowledgeably. 'He chews it the day long. The stench gets everywhere. Driving me insane, it is.'

'Oh.' I could see a butterfly flutter doubtfully across his face. He made a movement of his hand as though to brush it away.

'It's just garlic,' I said.

There was one good thing about Joe Maloney's staying with us: he seemed to understand the urgency of my need to clean the place up, and he appeared to take it seriously enough.

In his own way.

'We'll show 'em,' he said. 'We'll put up a fight. A conflagration. Show 'em they can't just trample on ordinary folk. With impunity, like.'

'Aye,' I agreed. 'We'll surely show 'em.'

I gritted my teeth with him, and together we set to

finishing the removal of all the rubble from the spare bedrooms.

When all the rooms were reasonably habitable, he said. 'That's enough dusting. Dusting's women's work.'

'What?'

'No, no, no, no. Don't get me wrong. I'm no chauvinist. It's just I was thinking. A lick of paint wouldn't go astray, like.'

'Paint?' I said.

'We could give the place a once-over. What d'you think, Nilus?' He was inspecting some woodwork, tapping it with his tradesman-like knuckles.

'Aye,' I said, assuming a returning business-like pose. My thumbs pressed into my trouser pockets. 'We could surely give it a once-over.'

Money, of course, was getting scarcer now, but we found a load of half-used paint tins in the basement. They were all different colours, leftovers from previous scattered renovations. 'We can mix it,' said Joe. 'Don't know what colour it'll turn out, but it'll do the job. You need a new coat of paint every once in a while. To preserve the plaster. You with me?'

'Aye, I am.'

We lugged all the old rusting cans up to the upstairs hall. It was a morning's work just getting started.

'That smell,' he said. 'Garlic, is it?'

'Yes,' I said. I could curse my father. Why was he always so embarrassing?

'Very strong. Anyway. Let's get down to business.' I could tell he was really anxious to work. 'You begin that end,' he said, sizing up one of the walls. 'I'll start here. Whoever gets to the middle first makes the tea.' He winked at me.

I didn't know what sort of bargain he thought that was, or what manner of a fool he took me for, but I did do my fair share. Of work, if not of the wall. He was a touch too impetuous for me. And when I stood back and stared at the finished painted wall that evening, I could see that the foot-wide strip I had painted was certainly executed a shade more expertly than his eleven-foot-wide expanse.

'It's a peculiar shade,' I said.

'Yeah. Wonder what you'd call it?'

'Puce, I think. Pale puce.'

He started rinsing the brushes in the landing bathroom. I watched, knowing I would have to clean and re-polish the basin after him, when he wasn't looking. 'We'll soon have this place licked,' he said.

I nodded a sort of wary agreement. He probably noticed this.

'Always clean your brushes, Nilus. The mark of a good worker.'

He was too useful at the moment for me to point out to him that I wasn't a worker of any shade or quality, and had no intention ever of becoming one. I let him get on with it.

'Does your father spend his whole time in his bed?' he asked over supper.

'He does now,' I said.

'Shame. Maybe I should just pop in, like. I'd like to thank him. You know, for letting me stay here. When Ira kicked me out, I was genuinely lost for a while.'

I considered this for a moment. But the risks were too high. In my father's present sideways disposition, God only knew what he might say. He might order the man off the premises. He might offer him garlic and frighten him away, willy-nilly. He might insist on speaking Italian, or try out a rosary even. It was far too dangerous. 'He doesn't really take to visitors,' I said.

'Tire him, do they?'

'Yes,' I said. 'They tire him.'

'Shame that. I'd like to shake his hand, you with me? He's doing wonders here. Keep the bastards at bay. That's what I say. He's a great man, your Da is. One of my heroes. Now, anyway. You proud of him? Know what I mean?'

As a human being, I found him – know what I mean? – resistible. But he was handy enough with a paintbrush.

As soon as he arrived, I could tell that the others in the house, Mrs Houlihan in particular, didn't quite take to Joe.

'He's worse than one of them mad poets forever sounding off in my ear,' said Mrs Houlihan to me privately.

I had no idea what she was talking about, save she mentioned poetry and poets more and more often these days – sort of disparagingly, as if she despaired of the modern Muse and the direction it was taking.

'Poets?' I said.

'They come to me under oak trees mostly,' she added. And she gave me a look that said she didn't understand it either.

Whatever, she and the other guests tended to make themselves scarce when Joe was around. When we'd finished a hard day's painting and decorating, we'd amble downstairs, and one by one, the others would make their excuses, with shame-faced looks, and we'd be left on our own.

'He's that sort of chappie,' said John Mitchell, 'would run you over in an ambulance.'

'The class of bolshie would kick a dog privately,' added Father Mulcahy, his eyes swinging like a nervous pendulum, 'when the dog was all but down.'

In the evenings, so, we were left to our own devices.

'Take Ira, for instance,' said Joe.

'Ira?'

'You know, your cousin.'

'What about Ira?'

'She went to Uni. Know what I mean? University.'

'Oh.'

'She did politics. Before she dropped out. That's how we met. Some picket line or other. She was all right, then. She was positive. She was on the right side. Committed, like. I was in love with her.' He fiddled with his spoon in his mug for a while. Then, 'For Chrissakes, I was in love with her!' he said.

It always amazed me about these tradesmen-like people that all they ever wanted to do was talk about themselves. Maybe tradesmen-like people was a touch unfair. Business-like people were as bad. My uncle, my aunt. All they ever wanted to do was talk about themselves, and their own problems. As if there wasn't a big wide world out there, slowly cracking up.

'What gets me is, you can live with a girl, a woman, two year and more, live with her day and night, sleep in the same bed, so you can, for Chrissakes, you can give her a baby even, and still not know her. Not properly, like. She can still turn round and boot you in the balls. When you're not looking.'

When he drank tea, he was very sloppy about it. He took three spoons of sugar, and stirred it endlessly. Inevitably, he'd have poured too much milk into the mug, and great dollops of it would spill on to the table. I was forced in the end to run around after him with a secret dishcloth, wiping surfaces wherever we ventured.

'She doesn't want to know me. I'm just a working-class Joe – to her. Underneath she's just like her Da. You know. Like your Uncle Frank. You know he was like that? He fought for socialism, too. For a year, maybe two. Soon gave it up. Still votes Labour, he says. Labour. Bloody capitalists. Their suits and all. Cars. Homes. Ira. Ah, she's a flirt. Flirts with the proletariat. Flirts with politics. With art – d'you know she hangs out at the theatre now? You know that?'

I didn't know that. And I couldn't see how it mattered where she hung out – know what I mean?

'You've been following her around?' I said.

Shame-facedly, he replied, 'I bump into her. Occasional, like.'

When I was bringing my father his supper tray, I passed Father Mulcahy on the stairs. He was muttering to himself.

'The reds go under the blacks,' he was saying, reminding himself, I presumed, how to play patience properly.

I sighed. It was hopeless.

'And the blacks go under the reds,' he mumbled, making his way to the breakfast room.

I gave my father his supper tray and sat down on the coverlet. I was listless. 'I don't know, Dad,' I said. 'Don't you get bored just lying in your bed all day?'

'Why should I be bored? Don't I have things cosy enough here?'

'Really?'

'Everything's at my fingertips. A bed to lie in, a bed to get out of.'

I could see what sort of a mood he was in. 'But Dad! I think I'm bored!'

But he was in full flow. 'The night to sleep in, the day to wake to. A sky to water me, a ground for inhumation. Could I ask for more?' He was inspecting his supper tray. 'Well, perhaps a brown bread bap or two.'

'Are you being serious, Dad?'

'God preserve me!'

'So you're joking?'

'God preserve me!'

The smell of garlic was too much at close quarters. I had to move away. 'Joe Maloney keeps going on about things. I don't know what.'

'Does he now?'

He scrutinized the food on his tray. I don't know, I thought. Everything these days, every action, looked disparaging.

'Why doesn't Uncle Frank come here any more?' I asked.

'Why don't you invite him?'

'We don't have a telephone, of course. God alone knows where I'd find a public one working, round here. And I'm not traipsing all the way to Killiney Hill.'

'Come on, Nilus. You know damn well he's here every day virtually.'

'Here? Don't be stupid. He's never here. My uncle? Sure, he's dead frightened of you. Isn't he?'

'He's outside, of course.'

'Outside?' I turned involuntarily towards the door.

'Yes. He's banging on the door. Virtually every day.'

'Doing what?'

'Oh Nilus,' said my father. 'What d'you think he's doing? Delivering milk?'

It was a stupid question. We hadn't had a milk delivery in years.

I started going through the dictionary again. Brainchill? Could there be such a word? Brain, yes. Chill, yes. But what would the two together mean? I knew very well what it meant, the word I was looking for. It meant that feeling you have when, I don't know, your brain goes all tense, no something else, intense – No, not your brain. Something else, I don't know, inside.

Brainchill?

At school my best subject had always been English. Or, to be more precise, comprehension. When they tested me at the age of ten, they found I had the reading age of a seventeen-year-old. They looked at me surprised. No wonder, I thought. Didn't I have the letters from my father to my mother to practise on? They made, it has to be said, fairly educative reading.

I wondered was it in them that I'd come across this difficult word, this brainchill? I searched through.

No brainchill.

I felt depressed, then. It was never easy reading how my father had planned my destruction. How fragile was life. It was only an accident that I had been born at all. Only an accident.

Anyway, the bulldozers outside were finishing work for the day. It was five-thirty, time for Disturbance.

Joe was away much of the time. When I asked where, he made up some ludicrous story of a strike in the perfume works down the road.

'Strike?' I said.

'D'you not know? Thought everyone'd know that.'

'It must be a fairly ineffectual strike,' I said. 'The perfume works was closed down years ago.'

He was busy putting his ex-army coat on. It seemed to have millions of straps and buttons and zips. 'How d'you make that out?'

'Well, just look at the entrance. Down the end of the street. It was bricked up I don't know how long ago.'

'You joking, Nilus?'

'No, I'm not joking. I watched them brick it up.'

'Sure, that was only when the ringway was built.'

'What was?'

'They moved the entrance, of course. To the ringway. You're having me on, aren't you, Nilus? You didn't really think it was closed down?'

I didn't know what I thought.

'Anyway, I'm off to support the comrades. Bleeding capitalist pigs.' He paused. 'I don't know. Sometimes you wonder – what's the point? I mean, what's the point? I mean –' He didn't seem to know what he meant. 'I met Ira yesterday,' he said.

'Oh.' I was too busy reeling at the news of the perfume works to take much interest in his wayward peccadilloes.

'She says to me, she says, "There's more to life than politics." That's what she said. "There's more to life than politics." You listening to me?'

'Yes,' I said quickly. 'There's more to life than politics.'

He gave me that queer look again. 'Well, yes,' he said. 'Of course there is. Of course there's more to life than politics.' He shrugged. He appeared for a moment to have forgotten what he was doing, where he was going. He frowned at the ex-army coat he was wearing. It must have reminded him. 'Anyway. Back soon. You with me?'

I had to follow him out on to the front steps to make sure that the bulldozers and cranes really were knocking down the cottages. I couldn't be sure of anything these days. Everything was topsy-turvy. Maybe the whole street was there the way it had always been. Maybe I was inventing things. Imagining them even.

The street certainly looked different. In the end there could be no doubt about it. There were spaces in the street where previously there had been homes. I felt sort of gratified.

I had been right.

I sought out my father, circumventing expertly the showers of plaster caught in odd sunbeams and the fracturing furniture on the way. I was a bit of a daydreamer, I knew. I often got the wrong end of the stick. But still.

I confronted my father in his bed in his bedroom. 'Why did nobody think to tell me the perfume works wasn't closed down at all? I've just made a terrible fool of myself.'

'Nilus,' said my father, almost groaning with some exasperation or other. There were pale slips of garlic skin stuck to his upper lip. So many, that his lips no longer looked red, but bloodless and cracked. 'You were always one step ahead of everyone else. Trouble is you're always travelling in the opposite direction.'

I found Mrs Houlihan in the kitchen.

'That Joe Maloney –' I began.

But she thwarted me. 'Don't be talking to me. I've had that lot up to me ears, so I have. Hardly catch a half-decent night's sleep without some versifying patriot on and on at me.'

She was off again. It was like one of those *aisling* poems we had to do at school, in Irish History class. Except she seemed to have got it wrong somehow. In school, it was always the patriotic poet who fell asleep, and the old ridden hag was supposed to come to *him* in *his* dreams. 'What do the poets say to you?' I enquired.

'Oh,' she replied. 'On and on they go about Spanish wine. Must think I'm some sort of alcoholic.'

'Doesn't sound much like something Joe Maloney would do,' I said doubtfully.

'Oh, he's no different. Save he hasn't the way with words, perhaps, that others might have. Okey-dokey. How's about chipped spuds and ham? That's what a young man likes. Chipped spuds and ham.'

I watched her peeling the potatoes. She had rings on her fingers now. Loads of them. I had no idea where they had all come from. They were like rings my mother used wear. Or not wear, exactly. Just keep in her locked drawer in her room. The same drawer the letters came from. From time to time, if it was raining or something, I used to pinch her key, just so's I could gaze at her jewels. They used to sparkle.

Anyway, Mrs Houlihan was less and less the tradesman-like person I remembered from the cottage down the street. She was turning more and more into a gypsy.

'Joe Maloney says we should forget about the boarding-house, and turn the place into a commune,' I said.

'Sure, it's nearly that now, with all my waifs and strays.'

'Yes.' I laughed with her. I was in a good mood. I didn't know why.

On my way upstairs, I heard John Mitchell playing his piano accordion. I battled through the rubble Mrs Houlihan and I had excavated from his room, then knocked on his door.

'It's Niall Moore, isn't it?' he said, eyeing the space above me and to my right in his usual surprise.

'I've come for my lesson.'

'Come in, so. Come in, so. Sit you down. Sit you down.'

The piano accordion was unexpectedly heavy. I found it difficult to balance it on my knees, never mind endeavour to play the thing as well. But he was patient enough. After an hour, I had a C major chord off nearly pat.

'That's enough for your first lesson,' he said. 'That's enough for today.'

He took the machine from me and began running his fingers caressingly over the keyboard. It looked as if he was reassuring them, the keys. As if he was saying, 'Don't you worry, my darlings, that young laggard won't be at you again in a while, my little darlings. Don't you fret.'

I should have been annoyed. Except there was some sort of lost elegance to his movements. I was quite touched really.

'Play me something,' I said.

He played some old tunes. 'The Mountains of Mourne' was the only one I even half-recognized.

'Where did you lose your sight?' I asked when he'd finished his medley.

'Lose my sight?' He looked so puzzled I wondered for a moment had he forgotten he was blind. 'In the Troubles,' he said eventually. 'Way back in the Troubles.' He sighed. 'For why, I don't know. It was all jigs and reels after that. Nobody wanted the good old tunes. Jigs and reels. That's all anybody wanted. Afterwards. After the Troubles. I don't know why I bothered. All jigs and reels. I lost my sight in the service of Ireland. And into the bargain, sure, I fought myself out of a living. Sure, I can't play jigs nor reels.'

Ira came around one day. She was very pregnant. I was worried she might burst on the breakfast room carpet.

'Drink,' she said. 'I want a drink.'

Joe looked anxiously at me. He wiped his hands on his dungarees.

'I don't think there's any drink here,' I said.

'Come on, Nilus,' she said. 'I saw a crate of brandy in the hall.'

'That's for my father.'

'You saying he wouldn't spare his poor pregnant niece a drop of the hard stuff? And she a poor unmarried mother-to-be. Come off it.'

She sat down on a stiff-backed chair. It was a difficult manoeuvre, like one of those games you can buy where you have to balance an awkward ball in a tight corner.

The chair wobbled when it received her bulk. I watched a cloud of dust rise, unsettled by her descent. My God, I thought, even the furniture in the breakfast room was dicey now.

'Where is he?' she asked.

'Who?'

'Uncle Phil, of course.'

'He's in his bed,' I said. 'Of course.'

'He's still the same?'

'What d'you mean?'

'I'm only asking after the health of my uncle, Nilus. You can keep your hair on. I might go up and see him after.'

'He doesn't take to visitors,' said Joe.

'You mean, he doesn't take to *you* visiting,' said Ira.

'He's probably asleep, anyway,' I said. I might have added: or ranting on in Italian, or telling rosaries, or wandering around naked, quoting from his *Teach Yourself Psychology* books and stinking the house out with his garlic. Or any other of the myriad manifestations of his sideways disposition.

'Anyway,' said Ira. 'About that drink.'

I left them to get some brandy from my father's stock.

When I returned, Joe was kneeling on the floor beside her, with his hand on her stomach. The pair of them made a most unattractive couple.

'It was a kick!' said Joe. 'I felt it. It's kicking away.'

'Of course it was a kick.'

'It's a baby,' said Joe. Unnecessarily, I thought. 'A real baby.'

'Of course it's a baby.' She took a swig from the glass I gave her. 'And guess whose baby it is?'

Joe sat down then. 'No need to pile it on,' he mumbled.

'And look at you,' she said. 'In your blue dungarees.

Paint splashed on them. Don't tell me you've got yourself a job.'

Joe said nothing.

'And tell me, whereabouts d'you keep your Armalite in that rig-out?'

'All right, you've had your fling. Now leave it off.'

'That's lovely talk for you. Drink someone, please.'

'Don't you think you've probably had enough?' I said.

She looked at me startled. 'Nilus, you've just mumbled half an opinion. Is it the end of the world next?'

'Don't mind her,' said Joe. 'She's just acting ignorant.'

'Ignorant, am I? What about men? That's what I want to know. Men! There's my father lounging away in his arm-chair, blaming my mother, just blaming my mother. "I used to have my principles, Ira," he whines away. "I used to have my dreams. But I gave them up for your mother. I gave them up for your mother and a decent home for you." And he goes and chooses my name for me. Ira. I – R – bleeding A. God, what a joke.'

'People change,' said Joe, quietly for him.

'Change? Damn right they change. One minute Daddy's a raving socialist, the next he's kicking a whole street out of their homes. His twin brother too. To build offices, I ask you. I changed. I thought you were the best thing since unsliced bread, so I did. Look at me. I'm carrying your bloody child, so I am.'

'Don't get all excited.'

'What the fuck do you care if I lose my baby? What the fuck does Joe Maloney care?'

Joe said nothing. I felt I should do something. I refilled her glass.

'I know, I know, I know I'm a bitch,' she said.

'You're not,' I said. I didn't know why.

'I am.'

'You're not.'

'I am.'

'She is,' said Joe.

'Thank you very much Joe bloody Joker.'

Joe glared at her, then flinched. 'Okay, I'm sorry. I'm sorry, Ira. Ira?'

'But you don't change, do you Joe Joker? You just carry on. Through thick and thin, good old Joe, reliable old Joe, he'll stick to his guns.'

'Maybe.'

'Maybe?'

'There comes a point . . .'

'There comes a point, Joe?'

'I don't know.' But it seemed he did. 'You wonder if your old man – one day when he wasn't a kid any more – I don't know – on a picket line, maybe, and it's raining, and the men are playing cards, and they're the same faces – up and down the country, everywhere you look, the same faces – they could be in ancient photographs – you just wonder did he decide to spend his life happy with Agnes, making Agnes happy, or would he continue seeking to change the world.'

'And?'

'And?' repeated Joe. 'And nothing. Just, oil and water; the two won't mix.'

I could tell from their faces that there was going to be a long silence. I was sick of this now. I had already stood up. 'Look,' I said. 'Why d'you have to talk like this? Why d'you have to say things like this? There's a whole world out there and it's all cracking up. Cracking up. Why d'you have to talk about these things the whole time? Can't you see it's cracking up?'

'What?' said Joe.

'Just everything. Like – I don't know – like *brainchill*.' The word spilled out before I could stop myself.

'I'm worried about him,' said Joe to Ira, after a pause, as if I wasn't even there any more. 'I think he's living in a world apart.'

'Ah, Nilus just doesn't want to grow up. Do you, cousin Nilus? You just don't want to grow up.'

I left. I listened on the landing for the front door to close, signalling they were gone. Then I went to my father.

'Innocence,' my father chose to inform me, 'can be maintained by a selective use of curiosity.'

'Is that all you have to say?'

'Who's the mother of invention?' he asked, exhaling a generous whiff of garlic in my direction.

I scowled at his change of subject. 'Necessity,' I answered.

'Ah, but who mothered necessity?'

'I don't know. I'm talking about brainchill. I'm talking about the whole world cracking up.'

'Why, of course,' said my father, regardless, 'invention is the mother of necessity.'

I looked at his hands. His wrists and fingers were getting bonier by the day. I wondered was I pouring enough brandy over them.

That night, Joe Maloney didn't return home. I hoped he was gone forever. We had a peaceful evening round the turf fire, like we used to have before he came to disrupt my routine. Father Mulcahy played patience, Mrs Houlihan played tarot, John Mitchell played 'Nobody's Child'.

I ambled over to Father Mulcahy.

'Please,' I said, 'don't change everything. Do my portrait for me. Please.'

'Nilus,' he said. 'Nilus . . .'

Mrs Houlihan looked up from her tarot. 'Go on, Father,' she said, smiling that smile of hers. 'What harm?'

'Truly, Missus?'

'Truly, Father.'

He sighed. 'Well then, Nilus,' he said. He coughed, searching for his old gruff voice. Already he was looking taller, the way he used to look in his black clerical suit. 'Take off them glasses –'

He coughed again, like a man with consumption.

'Go on, Father,' said Mrs Houlihan.

'Truly, Missus?'

'Truly.'

'Well then, Nilus,' he began again, and in the twinkling of an eye – either his own, or Mrs Houlihan's, or even my own, I couldn't tell – his irresolution of late was transmuted to the absolution of old, and he commanded, all delicious gravel and cinders, 'Take off them glasses till I make an inspection. I'll have to see if you're fit before I waste a sketching on the likes of you. I won't sketch riff-raff, as you very well know.'

I snatched off my glasses.

'Open your legs wide, now, till I get a decent pose. And don't be grinning back at me. 'Tis serious business, this.'

I started playing with my zip. Pulling it up and down. I was so happy. We were back to normal. After a while, it occurred to me the motion of my hand on my zip was the same as for masturbation, up and down, up and down. I giggled a bit, wondering if Father Mulcahy had spotted that. It seemed he hadn't. He was just sketching. I was still pulling on my zip. I decided this was silly. I may as well go the whole slog. I took my thing out.

'May as well go the whole slog,' I said, fairly cheerfully, conversationally.

'May as well,' said Father Mulcahy, through deft strokes of his pencil.

I knew I was grinning. Inanely, probably. I said, trying to poke some sense through the grin, 'Why d'you just sketch the whole time? Why don't you – why don't you –'

'Go on,' said Mrs Houlihan. 'Help the poor lamb.'

I'd forgotten she was there. I'd forgotten all about her. I began to blush, but on the whole I felt I'd left it a bit late to be embarrassed.

'Truly, Missus?' said Father Mulcahy.

'Truly, Father.'

He put down his sketch pad. I was still going at it, frantic. I could hardly keep it up, never mind anything else.

'The coals of hell,' began Father Mulcahy in his delicious cindery voice, 'the coldest of them is red – red – iron-red hot. Hotter than the colour of a blood-red orange, or the taste of a chilli powder on the tip of your tongue.'

'Go on,' I said. 'Go on.'

'And when Onan spilled his seed, each sickly grey worm of it grew to be a – What d'you think?'

'I don't know.'

'A demon, of course.'

'A demon!' I said. 'Yes!'

'And 'twas vile the brood of them, their faces evil and vicious, disordered with it –'

'Disordered!' I said.

'With limbs fierce as the red bar on the electric fire if you only whispered your cheek upon it.'

'Please, go on! You have to keep going!'

'And in the special deepest circle, the most particular circle of hell with the deepest and dirtiest dungeons of all, full of filth and smut all rubbled together, the place where your only supper is the vomit you vomited the night before –'

'Hurry up!'

'The place where you're heading, young Nilus Moore, if you continue in your evil ways –'

'Yes, Father! Yes, Father!'

''Tis there them demons of Onan's seed, they'd whip an evil boy like you with their electric limbs, and whip him justly –'

'Yesss!' I could only whisper now. 'Whip him jusssstly!'

'So that afterwards even the red hot, iron-red coals'd be a comfort to you, you evil, evil, evil boy.'

I came in a meagre dollop on my hand.

'Afterwards,' repeated Father Mulcahy, deflatedly.

I closed my eyes. I was exhausted.

'What's going forward?' said John Mitchell.

'Poor lamb,' said Mrs Houlihan. 'Sure he's whacked out. Okey-dokey, time for beddie-byes. Poor lamb, he's half-asleep as it is.'

I went to wash the sickly greyish sperm from my hand. I'd read something somewhere about the sperm count in the average human male being only half what it used to be. I didn't know why I was thinking about that. It was another thing to worry about.

At the wash basin, I wondered what I was supposed to be doing. I couldn't find any sperm on my hand. I turned my hand over and over and over. I held it against the light, I searched it in the mirror. Nothing. Not a blot. My hand was cleaner, purer, than a blank sheet of white paper.

I wondered what I was doing.

I walked down the street one evening to inspect the bricked-up entrance of the perfume works. Actually, I'd been pleased when the works had folded. Living in a street of tradesmen-like cottages was bad enough. I could certainly do without perfume worksmen toing and froing, morning, noon and night, with their delivery trucks and stench.

Except now it turned out the perfume works hadn't folded at all. They'd just moved the entrance when the ringway was built. And anyway, looking around that evening, I perceived that I no longer lived in a street of tradesmen-like cottages at all. There were still one or two left standing. But, in reality, I now lived in a demolition site. And our own house standing tall and gaunt against the grey evening stratus was like the one tree remaining on a blasted heath.

I'd been kicking loose stones against the bricked-up entrance. I suddenly wished I hadn't. I wondered should I pick through the kicked stones, replace them – if only approximately – where they'd rested, probably in peace, for years before.

Joe Maloney didn't return. I presumed he'd been picked up by the guards, for his agitation or something.

But Ira did return. She arrived late one evening in a taxi, with a million bags and the balloon inside her dress bigger than ever.

'Nilus,' she said, 'you've got to help me. I can't stand it at home. Not any more. With Mum fussing about, and Daddy going over the top about Joe – I just can't take any more of it.'

'What d'you want me to do?' I'd opened the door wide at first, but seeing who it was I closed it again to a peep.

'Well, I want you to put me up, of course.'

'Put you up?'

'You've got plenty of space here, haven't you?'

'Not plenty.'

'You've got a spare bedroom, at least.'

'I don't know.'

'Nilus, let me in off the street, at least!'

Reluctantly, I let her in. 'I suppose you think I'm all grown-up now.'

'What?'

'What you said to me last time you were here.'

She dithered with understanding me. Then she giggled in her old manner. 'Oh Nilus, is that all it is?' She dropped her bags. 'Go and put the kettle on, for God's sake. Here am I, up to my chin in family rows and unwanted pregnancies, and all you're worried about is some little nothing I said weeks back.'

I put the kettle on.

'Why were you arguing about Joe, anyway?'

'Just Daddy going on.'

'But I thought you didn't like Joe.'

'Don't be bonkers, Nilus. Joe's the father of old stinker here.'

I couldn't see the relevance of that, but I let it pass. Logic had never been Ira's strong point. That whole family seemed to treat logic as some sort of box of chocolates you could dip into when the mood took you. But mostly they were on a diet.

'Look, Nilus, d'you mind if I slip straight up to bed? Old stinker here is a bit of a bellyful, carrying him around.' She patted her stomach. 'Which bedroom can I sleep in?'

'I suppose,' I said, 'you can use the room Joe was in. I don't know if he left it tidy.'

'Joe's room? That'll be nice. I miss him, you know. It'd be nice to have, I don't know, the sniff of him around me. By the way, what is that smell?'

I sighed. 'Never mind,' I said.

She was already asleep when I brought her her tea. It was strange looking at her. There was a baby inside her. Kicking, by all accounts. A baby in the bed would take up such tiny space, even with the mother beside it. And yet the way she was now, the blankets barely covered her.

'Ah, the poor lamb,' said Mrs Houlihan, when I brought her up to peep. 'Of course, you must let her stay.'

'I wonder now, will it be a baby boy?' said Father Mulcahy, venturesomely. 'And what name they might give him so?'

John Mitchell played his accordion softly that night. So softly, you could hardly pick up the notes.

Next morning, Ira said she was tired after all the upsets of yesterday – apparently, she'd had a row with both her parents, a different, oppositional one with each. She said she wanted to stay in bed all day.

'Like my father,' I said.

'Yes, how is Uncle Phil?'

'Going strong.'

'There's something in this house going strong, whatever it is. Terrific smell. I might pop in and say hello later. If I feel any better.'

'Yes,' I said.

'By the way, I'd like to keep it quiet that I'm here. From my parents. Just for a day or two. I want to be on my own.'

'Yes,' I said. 'Sure.'

I was progressing quite well now with the piano accordion. I had nearly all the chorus of 'Nobody's Child' learned off by heart.

'Was that you playing the squeezebox?' said Ira, later that day.

'Piano accordion,' I corrected her.

'"Nobody's Child", was it?'

'You recognized the tune?'

'Your mother used play that one, didn't she? On the old squeezebox. When we used come here on Christmas Day. She'd have you up on a stool too, warbling away along with her. "I'm nobody's child., I'm no-o-body's child." Bet you used to hate having to sing that. Especially with the rest of us half-plastered with the drink. Ow!' Her assault on me and my mother ended in a condign moan.

'What's wrong?'

'It's a pain. I get it in my side sometimes. It's old stinker here at his gymnastics. When it comes, it hurts like – I don't know. Like a hot poker in the wrong place.'

Not hot enough, I thought as I left.

I told my father about Ira. 'Ira,' I said. 'Your niece. Ira. She's pregnant. With that joker's child. She's not even married. She's going to have a baby.'

But I could tell he wasn't interested.

'Of course you're not interested,' I said. 'A baby. A baby, remember? I've got the letters. I told you.'

That stirred him. 'Oh Nilus,' he said, sighing out the words, 'you never understood your mother's death, did you?'

This, of course, was quite wrong. The term before she died, we did eschatology in RK class.

126

Bright and early, the next morning, I brought Ira some tea. She was sobbing away.

'It's Joe.'

'What about him?'

'I miss him. Poor Joe. I miss him so much. I do, Nilus, I do.'

They had a very peculiar relationship, I thought. One minute they were at each other's throats, fighting like Kilkenny cats, drinking, sulking, splitting up. The next, she was crying because she missed him.

'I just wish I knew where he was.'

'Maybe,' I suggested, 'they've sent him to gaol.'

'Gaol? Why'd they do that?'

'Because he's an agitator, of course.'

'Don't be bonkers. Joe wouldn't hurt a fly.'

'You said yourself he carried an Armalite.'

'That was irony, Nilus. Irony. It's a method of argument. A method of persuasion, for God's sake. It's a refinement.'

'Oh. Very refined.'

'Joe wouldn't have anything to do with that crowd.'

She'd stopped crying now. I'd obviously brought her out of herself. I felt quite pleased, successful.

As soon as I'd finished thinking that, of course, she burst into a new sobbery. She was that perverse.

'Oh, I hope they haven't sent him to gaol. They haven't, sure they haven't?'

I checked my handkerchief was clean, then gave it to her. She dried her eyes.

'I'm being so silly.'

I considered saying, 'No you're not being silly.' But I couldn't work out if that was what she wanted to hear.

'Still, he'll come back to me. I know he will. And we can start all over again. Just the three of us.'

'Three?'

'Joe, me and old stinker here.'

'Yes,' I said. 'Just the three of you.'

She nodded. Her nodding was affirmative. She said, 'Yes, you're right.' At the same time, she was holding back a new flood of tears. I could guess what these tears, had they come, would have said. They'd have said something like, 'No, it's wrong! I want him here now! I want him with me now in this bed!'

Oddly, this contradiction didn't annoy me. I didn't think, 'The dithering idiot, she doesn't know what she's on about.' Instead, I caught myself wondering if she might be more than just a cousin, a cousin I was stuck with, whose purpose in life was to kick sand in my face, physically when I was younger, metaphorically now. For the first time, it occurred to me she might be motivated by feelings that had nothing whatever to do with me, were independent, indeed, of my existence. She might be a sovereign, if still difficult, woman.

I had difficulty with other people. I was as uncertain of them as, when a child and I closed my eyes, I was concerned that the world did, or it didn't, disappear. There was a word that described this feeling. Brainchill, was it?

I looked at Ira. She was still half resolved on cheerfulness, half on crying. One hand cupped her tea, the other straddled her belly. She had a pleasant face, quite orderly really. Everything was in its correct position. It was like the face on a clock. And her pageboys curls could be a black alarm bell nestling on top. I wondered if I liked her. I had a feeling I was starting something. It was dangerous territory.

'Don't worry about anything,' I said. 'You can stop here as long as you like.'

Much of the time she spent in bed. But sometimes I caught her drifting about in the upstairs hall. How, in her elephantine condition, she could manoeuvre herself between the rubble was beyond me. And not only the rubble. The hall had more the appearance of an obstacle course now, with all the half-used paint pots scattered about that Joe hadn't bothered to clear away and which now, I supposed, would become one more feature of the dilapidation everywhere around me.

When I'd confront her, she'd always make some play about the lavatory or the bathroom. But I knew nobody could be that concerned with their toilet. Except me, of course.

'My father doesn't like visitors,' I said. 'I told you. They tire him.'

'Nilus, I'm only going to wash my teeth.'

Then I said, 'Can I come with you?'

'What is this, Nilus? Why're you always following me around? You're worse than a hungry mongrel.'

I just wanted to be with her.

I didn't know what to do. I decided to ask my father.

When I got to his room, though, I forgot what I'd come to ask him.

'I know you're growing up, Niall,' he said. 'You told me you were, last time we spoke. But you really don't have to grow senile with it. You're always so enthusiastic. Head over heels into everything.'

'You called me Niall.'

'Did I?'

'You know you did.'

He didn't say anything. I wondered what sort of a mood he was in. 'Why did you christen me Nilus?' I asked.

'What do you mean?'

'It's a dead awful name. You know I had no friends at school. You know everyone just laughed at me. Nilus, they called, Nilus.'

'I didn't choose the name.'

'Are you trying to blame my mother?'

'Not at all. We both of us agreed on Niall. You used always to be called Niall, Niall Moore.'

I had a feeling, then, that he was maybe right, but that I had somehow neglected to remember. 'Until you had to go and change it,' I said. I'd rarely thought about the name before. But suddenly its unorthodoxy really riled me.

'What you are saying, Nilus? Sure it was you changed it. Don't you remember when you first went to senior school? You fell head over heels with your new subject. Latin, remember? We never sat to table any more, but you insisted we came to the *mensa*.'

'*Mensæ*,' I said abstractedly. 'Dative.' I wondered if I did remember this.

'You know what you're like, Nilus. You go head over heels into everything. You wouldn't answer us after that, unless we called you Nilus. Religion was the same. Remember after I had my first stroke? There wasn't a moment's peace but you had to drag me to one Mass or another.'

'I was worried about you,' I said. 'I wanted to do something. I wanted to help. But there was nothing I could do. I thought, I don't know, that maybe God would help you.'

'I'm not complaining, Nilus. It's just the inconsistency of it. I've often thought that. For someone as obviously predictable as you, you're so inconsistent. You know? Of course you know.'

I poured an entire bottle of brandy over him. Then I left

him to his garlic stench and his sideways disposition. There was no sense in him any more. It was as if he had a mission to tell me everything. A mission to confuse.

One morning I woke up early, as usual. I checked on my jigsaw. It was far too early actually to *play* Disturbance. But still I liked to check on the flat matt surface. Sometimes it glistened. Sometimes it was nearly reflective. You could nearly see your face in it. Cracked by the thousands of jagged lines. Sometimes.

Then I checked on my sheet-folds. They were up to standard. Then, when I'd cleaned the breakfast room fire, and brought in some more turf, and brought Ira her morning tea, I went outside to check on the bulldozers. They hadn't started yet. But sometimes they were late in starting. With my morning's chores done, I decided I could allow myself the luxury of half an hour's Disturbance.

But I couldn't. My Aunt-Agnes-stroke-Auntie-Nessie, walked right round the back of the house, straight into the kitchen, without knocking. Too late, I realized I'd forgotten to lock the back door after me.

'Nilus,' she said. 'I thought there was no one in. I've been knocking for an age on the front door.'

'The bell's broken,' I said.

'But I was knocking, Nilus.'

'I didn't hear you.'

She looked around the kitchen. Her ruffled look calmed to one of surprised satisfaction. 'My, you have been busy. I thought this place would be in a terrible state by now.' She ran a finger along a surface, checked it. 'Not even dusty. You have been busy. Well.' She sat down. 'I won't say I'm not surprised. A lot of people would've said you didn't have it in you. But I'm pleased.'

'I suppose you want some tea.'

'Thank you, Nilus.'

I had a feeling I was always going to be making tea for this difficult family.

'It's nice to see something going right in the world. God only knows, you need a bit of good news. Once in a while. I sometimes feel God must have it in for our family. I don't know where we went wrong. I just don't know.'

I sat down opposite her at the table. She had an old woman's face. I remembered something from RK class. Her brow was ridden with lines, written with sin like a guilty Hindu. She's taken her hat off, the one with the brim at the back, when she came in. But she still had her plastic see-through raincoat on. She had the look of a woman who came to Armageddon, prepared for rain.

'Ira's gone. I don't know where. She hasn't telephoned. And that baby's due. Soon, anyway. I've tried the hospitals. I've tried everything, God knows I have.'

When she moved, the plastic of her raincoat let off an unsatisfying squeak.

'And your Uncle Frank, I don't know, he seems to blame me. He sits at home, these days, just brooding. Of course it's not natural, brother against brother. But it's not my fault. He says I've changed him. He says before he met me he had his principles. He says I turned him into an unscrupulous businessman. He says I did it. Ira had a row with him. She called him a capitalist something. I said that was just her beau talking. Then she had a row with me. She's gone now. And I don't know where.'

'Oh.'

Power is the wrong word. I had a feeling of clemency, temporarily withheld. My father had a favourite painting, an Italian prince of the Renaissance. He used to say, 'Look at your man,' when he showed me his books. 'All proud and just and ruling. Then after the drawing session he pops off to do a spot of torturing in the afternoon.' And I'd laugh because he laughed. Then I'd sneak off to find my mother.

There was no mirror in the kitchen. But I knew I was wearing the same face as the Italian Renaissance prince. It was sort of brainchilling.

My aunt was still talking.

'It was never easy, Nilus. I suppose you blame me too. But Nilus, did you never watch your uncle – you must have caught a glimpse at least – how he'd look at me laying his table. Did you never catch him say to himself while he watched me lay his table: "I gave it all away for the love of that woman"? And how he would smile saying it?'

I swallowed. It was difficult following her. She seemed to be all over the place.

'It made him feel so happy. I was the wife who would say "Nonsense, Frankie, have a chocolate," and he could tell himself, I came down to earth for the love of that woman.'

I began to worry about the kettle. Would it never boil? I needed to be doing something. I could feel the brainchill coming on.

'And you play out this little game over the years, you don't see it happening, but in the end you feel and act the way he wants you to feel and act and you say "Nonsense," and – good gracious – you mean it.'

The kettle whistled. I leaped up.

'And Nilus, it hurts after so many years of being the silly woman in your husband's life, it does hurt to suddenly look at yourself and think, for so many years I've been the silly woman in my husband's life.'

There was a pause then. I wondered if I was supposed to say something. The only thing I could concentrate on was her split infinitive in 'to suddenly look at yourself'.

'You see, I was his excuse. And now he's blaming me. And now my child has gone.'

'Er – Auntie Nessie –'

'Aunt Agnes, please.'

'Aunt Agnes, what are you . . .'

'Yes?'

'I don't know what –' I shrugged '– you're talking about.'

'I'm trying to explain everything to you, Nilus. I want you to know what's happening. I sometimes feel you don't listen. I'm putting everything down on paper for you. Black and white. This feud in the family has got to end.'

She tapped the table edge with her index fingertip.

'Feud,' I said. 'Yes.'

She didn't seem to be talking about Ira any more. I wondered should I get in my news now, before the subject was forgotten entirely, that her daughter was safe and well in one of the bedrooms upstairs. It was a serious problem. My aunt would be pleased. She'd be pleased with me. I'd be rid of Ira. And the difficulty of her.

But, on the other hand, I didn't know if I was finished with Ira. I wasn't sure if I liked her yet. I was worried about her child. It wasn't safe bringing babies into the world these days. Anything could happen. The letters in my bedroom told me that.

My aunt had an expectant look on her face. She'd asked a question. I couldn't remember what. 'No' was always the safest answer.

'No,' I said.

'It's not your father?' She looked disorientated.

Upstairs, the floorboards were creaking. I realized she must have heard them. Somebody was creeping around.

They creaked again.

'No,' I said quickly. 'I mean it *is* my father.'

'Nilus, can't I speak with him?'

I mimed doubtfulness. The brainchill inside me understood immediately that I hadn't finished with Ira. Not yet.

'Can't you get him even to talk to your uncle? If only people would talk.'

'He doesn't want to talk to anyone these days.'

'I know. They're both as stubborn as each other. But Frankie has at least tried. How many times has he been around here, knocking? Your father won't even open the door to him. Can't you have a word with your father? I know it's not your fault, Nilus. You're an innocent caught up in all this. But so am I. And this thing is ruining my marriage. It has got to end.'

'My father told me I am not to open the door to Uncle Frank,' I said firmly. 'He says Uncle Frank wants to demolish this house. It's crazy, I know. The cottages in the street are one thing. But this house is a home. It's my father's home. It's where my mother lived. It's where she died. My father says that Uncle Frank must never darken his door again.' I shrugged, resignedly. 'I'm sorry. Myself, I quite like my Uncle Frank. But there's nothing I can do to persuade my father.' I had spoken very straight, calmly but firmly. I'd listened to myself while I spoke. I sounded very adult. I sounded like someone else, or more, like a recording of myself. It was, yes, it was brainchilling.

'But Frank has bought you a beautiful new home. On the Hill. You'll love it there. Who would want to live here? This house is – is –'

'Brainchilling,' I said, then bit my tongue.

'Nilus?'

The word had slipped out.

'Nilus?'

'Aunt Agnes, *I* would love to live on the Hill,' I said, sadly. 'But my father won't move.'

'Should I speak to him?'

'No.'

'Very well.' She finished her tea. 'I tried. God knows, I tried.' She stood up. 'By the way, you'd better get that bell fixed. I had an anxious telephone call the other day. From your father's doctor. Apparently, he's been around trying to get in. Something to do with a two-monthly check-up. Your father, I mean. It's overdue. Says there's nobody answering the door.'

She didn't have to tell me about the bell. After all, it was I who had banjaxed it. 'Yes, I'll have to see to that.'

She kissed me as she was leaving. 'It's not easy for you, is it, Nilus? What do you do all day? It's holidays now, isn't it? School holidays. I suppose you watch television the day long. There's nothing else to do here.' She put her hat on. 'I'm just sorry, that's all.'

I double-bolted the door after her.

I raced up the stairs. I needed to play Disturbance. I needed to play it badly. The smell upstairs was dire. Overwhelming. But I'd expected that. My father's door was ajar. I stayed my feet. I walked in, casually enough.

'Ira's been in, hasn't she.'

'Yes,' said my father.

'What did she say?'

'Enough.'

'It's a shame,' I said.

'You knew she would.'

'I told her not to disturb you. I warned her.'

'You never stop to think, Nilus. Of the consequences, I mean. Letting her stay.'

I couldn't tell him that I was lonely. We didn't have that sort of relationship. 'I don't want to go into all that,' I said.

'Of course you don't.'

I poured some brandy over him.

'Why are you doing all this?' he asked.

'I'm not *doing* anything,' I answered. 'Doing is what I'm not doing. I'm *saving* things.'

'Saving what, for God's sake?'

'Order,' I said. 'Some semblance of order in this shambles.'

Ira was in my bedroom.

'You shouldn't be here,' I said.

'It's a shrine,' she said.

She was gazing at my table with the black jigsaw and the night candles always lit, flickering on the matt surface and on the framed photographs of my mother.

'It's a shrine,' she said again. She turned to me. 'Oh, Nilus, I never knew. I never knew what it meant to you. Nobody knew.' She had been crying. 'Why didn't you tell anyone?'

I really wanted to talk to her. I really wanted to talk.

I said, 'Nobody knew what?'

'Oh Nilus. You've got to come with me now. You're coming with me. Now.'

'Coming where?'

'I know what's going on here. I've seen – I've been to see – your – I know what's going on here.'

I put my arm around her. 'But Ira,' I said, wheeling her around towards the door and the stairs down from the garret to the lower bedrooms, 'there's nothing going on here. Myself and Mrs Houlihan are opening up the place as a boarding-house. That's all. It's to please your father, my uncle. We can't have idle buildings, you see. We can't have money pouring down the drain. That's all. You see, Ira, there's a simple explanation for everything. If only you look. My father calls it Occam's Razor. He was probably asleep when you looked in. He does look odd, when he's asleep, I know. Too much brandy probably. And garlic. But you need to rest now. You need to rest. Isn't that right, Ira? Of course that's right. You need to rest.'

She was surprisingly light, when I carried her. Or I was surprisingly strong.

I n the kitchen, Mrs Houlihan arranged a quick conference.

'Broth,' she said. 'That's what a young mother-to-be needs. Good strong broth. Okey-dokey.'

And we were all set our different tasks. Mrs Houlihan boiled up carcasses of old chickens, I did the relay to and forth, John Mitchell played quietly on his accordion.

'Only lullabies mind,' Mrs Houlihan admonished.

'And what about me?' said Father Mulcahy in his sickly moaning voice.

I looked at him. His face was empty. I stared for a long time, trying to find words for my distaste. But then I flinched. I shook my head. I felt ill at ease, unaccountably so. I looked at him again. It came to me in a flash why Father Mulcahy had changed. I felt quite pleased with myself. He had frightened me somewhat beforehand, with his harsh ways and intolerant manner. But now I was actually terrified of him. I could quake in my shoes at the mere thought of his empty mindless face. It was horrifying.

So that was why he had changed. I felt so happy. At last I understood. All was well. He was doing it to hurt me.

I looked up at Mrs Houlihan. She smiled her smile.

'Do you still pray, Father?'

'I do. A bit. Off and on.'

'Okey-dokey, you can do the praying.'

Father Mulcahy's face brightened. 'I'll pray for a boy,' he said. He looked for a second like one of his angels, the beautiful boys he'd told me about; the ones whom alone in all the world he would consider for altar service.

I shuddered.

While I was dawdling about in the hall that afternoon, waiting for four o'clock and my next legitimate assignation with Disturbance, I began to hear a strange noise. It was in the hall somewhere, but I couldn't quite detect its source. It was an insistent, clicking noise, rather like the ticking of a hollow clock. On and on it went, always in the back-ground, like the air itself was marking time. I got down on my knees on the threadbare carpet, to check was it coming from beneath the floorboards. I listened to the mouldings on the doorcase and jamb. I even tried the banisters. But the noise seemed not to be coming from any particular place. It was simply there, in the ether.

I sank down on to the bottom step of the stairs. I wasn't especially perturbed by noise. Our house was old, a century or more at least. It creaked with the wind and the passage of time. It was the metronomic clicking of this noise that was getting to me. I could feel it in my head, like a pulse in my temple, insistent, insinuatory.

Above me, some plaster had crumbled from the ceiling. I could just make out the planed edge of a joist showing through. I bowed my head. I was certain now where the noise was coming from, certain too of its portentous nature.

It was deathwatch beetle. The joists were riddled with it. And the tapping sound of the jaws, phalanxes of them no doubt, gnawing through the wood, the very vitals of the house –

'Presaged death,' I said aloud, quite resigned . . . 'Presaged death.'

Abruptly, the clicking stopped. I held my breath. The moments counted interminably. I felt myself huddled on the bottom step of an immeasurable staircase, and beneath me yawned all of oblivion.

And then the chimes came. For a moment I didn't bother even to look up. I imagined I was dreaming. But when, eventually, I did peek through my fingers, I couldn't believe what I saw. My hands slipped from my brow. I stared for ever and ever. I just couldn't believe it.

It *had* been the ticking of a clock, after all. Right in front of me stood the grandfather clock, the same piece, with its fake walnut veneer, that had stood there ticking since before I could remember. Somehow or other, I had completely neglected to remember anything about it. It had never occurred to me the mechanism might still be workable, never mind working. But it definitely was working. Its chimes had just struck four o'clock.

Could it be that I just hadn't noticed before?

I picked myself up, gathered myself together, brushed the carpet dust from my pants. So much for deathwatch beetles, I thought. But I wasn't too rankled. The state of this place, I allowed, would give any man a turn.

Then I remembered it was gone four o'clock. I dashed up the stairs. I was late for Disturbance.

In my bedroom, I stared for a long time at my jigsaw. It wasn't raining. It was quiet. Normally, I liked the quiet. But this was a thicker quietness than normal. Sort of waterlogged.

Maybe I still hadn't recovered from the start the grandfather clock had given me, but everywhere felt almost unnaturally silent.

I picked away at a corner, but it was so still, I couldn't concentrate. I left it. For the first time ever, I left my jigsaw willingly in the middle of a Disturbance. I wandered downstairs again.

In the hall I delivered a wary glance to the grandfather clock. It was still ticking, rounding its way towards five. I wondered who was winding it. Mrs Houlihan, probably, knowing her.

I opened the fake walnut door. I stopped the pendulum. That was better. Silence was one thing, but I could live without being reminded how long it endured.

'Do you spend your time watching television?' my aunt had enquired.

I'd forgotten all about television. I used to like television. The set was still in the breakfast room. I switched it on.

I was surprised to see it was a colour set. I'd forgotten that.

I looked around the breakfast room. For some reason, I didn't know why, our house looked all black and white. No, that was wrong. It looked grey. Everything was candescent, worked out in subtly varied shades of grey. Like cinders in a dead fire, or linen too often, or too little, washed.

The colour television glared out from its recess. It was a whole other world. I switched it off.

The thick silence engulfed me again. Something was happening. There was a word that described this feeling. Brainchill, was it? Or, maybe, it was that something wasn't happening. Maybe that was it. Something wasn't happening. There was a word that described this feeling. Brainchill, was it?

I had to go outside to check, but already I knew what it was. The bulldozers hadn't started that day. There was no background drone. Not even a rumour of them.

I peeped out through a bare patch in the hedge. The workmen were there. The bulldozers were there. But they were redundant at last. There were no more cottages left.

It was an ex-street.

I made a mistake then. I delayed outside too long. The garden gate creaked open, a guard breezed in. I tried to hide, but already it was too late.

'Hello there,' said the guard.

There was nothing for it but to saunter up to him, assuming his own breezy manner.

'Hello.'

'Phillip Moore,' he said. 'I'd like to have a word with him.'

'You can try,' I considered saying. 'I'm his son and even I can't get a decent sensible word from him.' But I didn't.

'He's sick,' I said. 'He's not to be disturbed.'

The guard was a bit put out by that. 'Sick? I have a signed order here. For his eviction.'

It was, of course, the most ludicrous thing I'd ever heard. The guard stood his ground. His accent told me he came from the country. He was a rednecked culchie. I considered dashing into the house and slamming the door in his ignorant face.

As it transpired, I didn't have to.

The remarkable thing was that my deliverer had been there all along, and I hadn't recognized him. A group of demolition men had gathered round the street gate, gobbing at the guard. A man detached himself from this group, walked up the drive, and turned into my Uncle Frank.

'Uncle Frank!' I cried.

'What's all this about, guard?' he said, ignoring me.

'Mr Moore,' said the guard. His attitude changed immediately. 'I have the eviction order here with me. Just like you asked. It's all signed now.'

'I see.'

'I hope now I haven't chosen an inconvenient moment,' said the guard. 'But my orders were 'twas urgent.'

'Not at all, guard. Not at all.'

They ambled away together, round the back of the house. They'd forgotten about me. I went inside and watched them from the upstairs windows. After a while, the guard came back round the front, chuckling to himself and shaking his head. He climbed into his car, radioed something, then drove away.

I found my uncle in the back garden. He didn't turn to face me. 'Well, Nilus,' he said, fairly lugubriously. 'It's come to a pretty pass.'

I sat down beside him on the little mound of grass that overlooked the canal. 'It sure has,' I said.

'I'd hoped it wouldn't come to this. Truly.'

'Yes. So did I.'

We sat in silence for a while. The grass was damp. I could feel it miring through the seat of my pants. But I knew I mustn't move. My uncle was staring at the slow water of the canal, at the scum on top and other people's litter floating by.

'How is he?' he asked.

'Not too bad.'

'Still of the same mind?'

'He won't change now.'

'He's gone stubborn in his old age. I suppose we both have. There's a jinx on this business. From the very beginning, there's been a jinx on this job. Ira's gone, did you know that?'

'My aunt told me.'

'And Agnes will address nary a civil word to me.'

'I know. She was here earlier today.'

'The thing is, of course, I've laid out so much money and investment on this project, to pull out now, 'twould ruin me. Totally. Bankrupt.'

'Yes.'

'And that joker of Ira's. You know he was trying to stir up trouble with the workers? I caught him agitating here to get the workers out on strike. In sympathy with the perfume factory. I tell Ira what a fool she was even considering that joker, and she flames off at me. That's what really upset me. She went off without saying anything, not even a by-your-leave. Her mother's half-frantic worrying. I decided then, I'd bloody get him. And I bloody did. And now I don't suppose she'll come home until or unless I drop the charges. What a mess.'

'What charges?'

'Well, I had to stop the joker. You can understand that, can't you, Nilus?'

'You mean he's in gaol?'

'Only temporarily. It'll do him no harm. A short sharp shock is exactly what he needs. Do him the world of good, the joker. Ira didn't even wait to hear, but disappeared. She was always headstrong, that one.'

I was busy smiling a secret smile. This was wonderful news. I wasn't a fool or a daydreamer, after all. My hunch had been correct. It took brains and brain power to work out a hunch like that. I'd told Ira her beau might be in gaol, and she'd laughed at me to my face. But I'd been right all along. This was wonderful news.

'And I suppose she won't come back now till I drop the charges.'

He fell silent for a while, a long while, his usual aeon. I began to feel all agitated. I wished now I hadn't so easily left my jigsaw in the middle of a Disturbance. That was wrong of me.

145

The water in the canal sort of scummed past. The canal hadn't been used for years since. Or else it was in constant daily use. I couldn't really distinguish those extremes any more.

Mrs Houlihan had said to me, 'Poor lamb, you're living in a meantime.'

'A meantime?' I'd said.

'A meantime.' And she'd given half an uproarious laugh . . .

I looked around the back garden. I wondered was it overgrown?

My uncle roused himself. 'Well, I suppose I'll have to do something.' He was about to stand up, but he stopped, sighed long and heavy, slumped down again. He ran his hand through the thin streaks of hair on his crown that he was training to cover his bald patch. 'What're we going to do about your old man?'

'God knows,' I answered, returning his hopeless tone.

'Poor Nilus. It's no fun for you, is it?'

'I'm all right.'

'You could come and stay with us, if you liked. On the Hill. There's plenty of room.'

'I'd like to, Uncle Frank. I'd really like to. But I don't think I could leave my father on his own. It wouldn't be fair.'

'You're a good lad, Nilus. Faithful to the last. I like that in a young man.'

He stood up, so I stood up with him.

'It's just that he really is sick, you know.' I shrugged resignedly.

He patted me on the shoulder. His pats got slower and heavier till in the end he left his hand rest there. 'We'll sort something out, with your father. He's my brother, after all.

My twin brother. Don't let it weigh on you too much, Nilus. We'll sort something out.'

He wheeled me round leadenly, and we walked in step back round the house towards the front drive.

By the side of the house, he started going on about seeing someone waving at an upstairs window. I thought for a moment. 'Oh, that'll be Mrs Houlihan,' I said.

'That mad old bag from down the road?'

I opened the street gate for him.

'My father brought her in to help with the housework.'

'But I heard she'd been carted off to Grange Gorman.'

I frowned, then shrugged. 'You must have heard wrong,' I said.

He got into his car. 'Yes. Anyway. Now, don't worry too much. I'll get this mess sorted out. We're a family. We'll all have to start behaving like that. A family.'

He left. The workmen were still crowded together near the street gate. I smiled at them, like I suffered from a sort of risus sardonicus.

I told Ira her father had been.

'I saw him,' she said. 'Nilus – '

'You don't have to worry, Ira. I didn't tell him you were here.'

'Nilus – ' she said again.

'Honest, Ira. I gave you my word. I won't tell anyone you're here. You shouldn't risk it at windows, though. I had to tell him it was Mrs Houlihan. That's risky, Ira. Very.'

'Nilus, you're sick – you need help.'

'Don't be silly, Ira. It's you who's sick. You're carrying a baby. It's due soon. I'm worried about it. Babies are dangerous articles. In fact, you shouldn't be up at all, Ira,' I said, as I helped her back into her bed. 'You need to rest. You've got to save your energy. It's not easy having a baby. You should see what it did to my mother. Life isn't easy, she used to say. And it really isn't. Giving it, especially.'

'Nilus, will you listen to me – '

'I'll be back later. I'll bring you some broth. And I'll introduce you to the other guests. You'd like to meet them, wouldn't you?'

'Other guests? Yes, Nilus, I'd like to meet them. Now, if I can. Why don't I meet them now?'

'No, no, no. They're all busy now. Mrs Houlihan is cooking up broth. John Mitchell is playing lullabies on his piano accordion. Father Mulcahy is saying prayers for the baby. He wants it to be a boy, you see,' I added in explanation.

'Nilus!'

'I'll be back later. I have a game of Disturbance to finish now.'

I passed Father Mulcahy in the hall. He was muttering to himself. 'The red goes under the black,' he was saying. I edged out of his way. I waited for him to close his door after him. I felt terrified, alive.

I had a quick word with my father.

'Your brother's been round.'

He didn't respond. I wanted to tell him how pleased I'd been with my uncle's visit. He hadn't talked about socialism. He hadn't talked about capitalism. Nothing like that. He'd talked about real things, my home.

'I don't know, Dad. You're not so cheerful these days. Are you not pondering on the futility of it all any more?'

My father roused himself slowly. 'You're yapping on,' he said, 'like a calf in a slaughter house. Have some garlic.'

I tried to think of something clever to say. At the back of

148

my mind there fluttered tantalizingly a thought both bril-
liant and witty. It would amaze my father with my wither-
ing insight. Unfortunately, it seemed to involve a word
whose exact articulation eluded me. Was it 'brainchill'
again? Could there be such a word?

I scratched my head in the precise place wherein lurked
the amazing thought. Then I burst out, risking it:

'Brainchill!'

My father's laughter was still ringing in my ears when
eventually I sat down quiveringly to contemplate
Disturbance.

Late that night I opened Ira's door, and in procession, the
four of us – Mrs Houlihan, Father Mulcahy, John Mitchell
and I – brought in her sustenance. I carried the broth.

'Here you are,' I said. 'Be careful. It's steaming.'

'Poor lamb,' agreed Mrs Houlihan. 'We can't have you
burning your tongue.'

'Now,' I said, 'I promised I'd introduce you to the other
guests, and here they are. This is Mrs Houlihan. She's the
one who cooked your broth for you.'

'Good strong broth, that's what a young mother-to-be
needs.'

'Mrs Houlihan?' Ira repeated. She looked around blindly
for a moment.

'Well, who'd you think it was?' said Mrs Houlihan,
'Róisín Dubh singing "*My Dark Rosaleen*"?' And she
laughed her riotous laugh.

'And this is John Mitchell. He plays the piano accordion.
He's giving me lessons. Ask him to play something for
you.'

'I don't play jigs and reels, mind,' warned John Mitchell
firmly. 'Get that straight, first of all. No jigs, and no reels
neither.'

'He won't play jigs and reels,' I added, backing him up.

'Nilus! Stop it! There's no one there! Just stop it!'

John Mitchell endeavoured to look surprised and dis-
mayed at the same time.

'And this is Father Mulcahy.'

'Ira,' said Father Mulcahy darkly. I'd got Mrs Houlihan
to rehearse him in this. ''Tis not a saint's name. There's no
Saint Ira.'

'And that's the three guests,' I said. 'Except, of course,
Mrs Houlihan isn't really a guest.'

'Not at all,' chimed in Mrs Houlihan. 'I'm more what
you might call a fixture here.'

'She sees to the cooking,' I explained.

'Okey-dokey,' said Mrs Houlihan. 'Time we all laid our
weary heads to rest. Okey-dokey.'

I opened the door, and the three of them trooped out.

'Goodnight, Ira.'

'Nilus,' she said. Her poor voice sounded terribly
strained. 'Please don't lock the door again.'

'Lock the door?' I said. Sometimes you could look at Ira
and see she wasn't – I don't know – she wasn't quite as
orderly as I'd thought. Sometimes she didn't look orderly at
all.

'I think I might take a little walk, Nilus.' She was shivering. 'Before I go to sleep. I just feel I'd like some fresh air.'

I gave her the benefit of a doubtful look; then switched
my face to a sad resolution. 'I'm afraid not,' I said. 'Mrs
Houlihan has said it's time to go to sleep. Of course, you
must feel at home here, Ira. But, well, Mrs Houlihan was
the first to arrive. She might get jealous.'

'Nilus!' she screamed.

I tucked her in, my hand over her mouth. 'Besides, my
father's such a light sleeper. Especially these nights. He

sleeps all the day, you see. The last thing he wants is doors banging open and closed the night long. So you understand,' I said, closing her door, 'why I have to lock you in.'

'Nilus!'

I turned the key.

'It's just my father,' I explained through the locked door of her bedroom. 'He's such a light sleeper.'

Mrs Houlihan was beside me when I turned. She had a candle burning low on a saucer. She was in her white shift, snow white, like she had beaten it with stones in a sun-drenched river. The candle-light caught the gold-coloured bull-nose rings in her ears and my mother's jewellery on her fingers.

'Okey-dokey,' she said. She had to speak quite loudly over the hammering and din coming from Ira's door. 'Do you want to come and kiss me goodnight?'

I followed her into my father's bedroom. She peeled back the sheet from my father's cadaverous body, slipped in beside him.

'Goodnight, Mrs Houlihan,' I said.

'Goodnight, Nilus.'

Even though she'd blown her candle out, I could still see her smile tarrying in the draughtless air.

'Goodnight, Dad.'

'Goodnight, son. Sleep well.'

The seasons colluded with events. Winter had come. At my high garret window I watched the rain drive against the panes. The arid heat from the electric fire rose sluggardly before me, to waft around my face when it reached the sills, whiffled by a draught, a mere fugitive of the wild winds that lashed the chimney stacks and slates beyond. Sometimes the rain came in waves, like regiments attacking a last fortress. I had a feeling that the translucent defences of my garret room, the two windows and the deadlight in the gable, outraged the season. Another gust would blow, whipping up the rain's ferocity, and I would listen as another slate clattered down the roof and watch as it fell to shatter on the ground. But the window panes held. I was safe inside, a while, and warm enough.

In my hands I held the letters. I didn't read them any more. Just kept them in my hands. That was enough. Their presence was in some way necessary, or half-necessary, or something. But not to read them. Like at Mass you don't actually need your missal, you know the thing off by heart, but still you bring it with you. It sort of explains why you're there.

Sometimes the banging downstairs in the bedroom below would falter a while, and then I would try my hand at Disturbance. But one way or another, the potency of the game was perishing. Now it felt as nearly dully ordinary as pulling away some pieces of a jigsaw and putting them back together again.

My sheets were perfect. The dust was at bay.

Nothing was happening. I was getting bored with that now. Nothing had happened so often lately.

I went to my father.

'Are the seasons colluding with events?' he asked me.

'Well . . . yes,' I answered, not understanding why he should snigger at me so.

'It's the meantime,' he announced.

'What is this meantime? Mrs Houlihan keeps going on about it. "You're living in the meantime," she keeps saying. "Poor lamb." What's it supposed to mean?'

'God knows,' said my father.

He hardly moved these days. It was difficult even to imagine him moving. Sometimes it was as if he wasn't even there.

'What?' said my father, disturbing my thoughts. 'Of course I'm here.' A shade of his sideways behaviour returned to his cracked grin. '*Foeteo ergo sum*, sure.'

'And what's that supposed to mean?'

'You're the one with all the Latin, Nilus.'

'Just tell me.'

'Roughly translated, "I stink therefore I am." '

I suppose it was funny. I couldn't help myself but laugh a little with him. I had to stop quickly, though. The stench of him was too much through an open mouth.

'I have the letters with me,' I said, experimentally. 'The letters you sent to my mother. When she was in hospital.'

'We've done the letters, Nilus,' he said. 'We went through them, one by one, ages back. The letters were explained long ago. After your mother died. Finished. Are you saying now you've forgotten that too?'

153

The smell was like a hundred garlics in a press uncleaned after a thousand cloves.

I suppose I did remember. It was just, what with one thing and another, I found it so difficult to concentrate these days.

'Poor lamb,' said Mrs Houlihan, when I sought her out. 'A couple of aspirin's no use at all. Not in your condition. Sure I know what's up with you.'

'What's up with me?'

'It's the banging, isn't it? Topsy-turvy banging everywhere.'

'Yes, it's the banging.' It really was the banging. I was surprised I hadn't worked that out for myself. 'It just never goes away, Mrs Houlihan. Never ceases, recedes, never stops. It's there the whole time. It gets me in my head, my skull, in my brain. It's sort of cold. Like a chill. The banging.'

'Poor lamb.'

'And sometimes it gets closer, nearer, more impending. Like now. The banging's down here now. I can hear it down here now. Incessantly, all the time, interminably.'

'And why don't you open the front door, so?'

'But I don't know who's out there, Mrs Houlihan, knocking, rapping, thumping on the front door.' I'd started this recently. Repeating words. No, not words. Just myself. Me, myself, muggins.

'Open it and find out, sure.'

I wondered should I risk it.

'I'll make myself scarce,' said Mrs Houlihan, as though it was the final temptation of a bargain offer.

I opened the door, and immediately wished, begged, craved that I hadn't. It was Joe Maloney.

'Jesus, Nilus,' he said, barging in. 'Thought there was no

154

one home, so I did. Thought everyone'd packed up and left.'

'Well, you were wrong.' Inaccurate and mistaken, I added to myself.

He insisted on tea, then on drinking it, then on me listening to him yapping on.

'I'm looking for Ira,' he said.

'Oh.'

'I've got to talk to her. I've got to – you know, Nilus – I've got to tell her. I've got to find her and tell her – know what I mean? – I don't know – that I – I really love her. I really love her. Like.'

I was thinking about Ira and her immanent baby. Then I thought about the letters.

Just after my mother's death, I'd confronted my father with the evidence of his murderous intentions. It all seemed so very very long ago.

'You see, Nilus,' my father had said, 'the doctors knew all along it was dangerous for your mother to give birth. Something about her womb, Nilus. She was always delicate, your mother.'

'Yes,' I had agreed at the time. My mother had always been delicate. 'Matchsticks for bones,' she used complain. 'Calcium. Your Grandfather's cows were always lazy with their milk.' I could see and hear her saying that, scrupulous at the sink, even now.

'Yes,' I said again to my father. But of course, it was Joe Maloney who heard me.

'Yeah,' he said. 'Of course you're right. It's just – you know – you don't see that sort of thing. Not when you're running around all day long. Not when you're busy and breathless on the helter-skelter of politics, like. But you're right. Ira is more important. She's more important than the whole world put together. The whole shooting-gallery. Her and her baby. Our baby. The three of us together: that's the only truly important thing. That's why I've got to find her.'

'And Nilus,' my father had said, in that reasonable voice he'd still used conventionally, shortly after my mother's death, 'I did urge her not to go ahead with it. Your birth. I did urge her. I make no apology. It's got nothing to do with you, really. And besides, you wouldn't know anything about it, would you – '

'No, I wouldn't know a jot. I wouldn't know anything if you'd had your way and I was murdered.'

'If you,' my father had continued in that relentlessly reasonable voice of his, 'if you hadn't stolen those letters from your mother's jewellery drawer – or if your mother hadn't kept them . . .'

'Oh yes, blame my mother!'

'What?' said Joe. He was still bloody there.

'Nothing,' I answered. *Niente, nihil,* I added to myself.

'It's just Ira,' he said. 'I love her . . .' He was off again.

'I even found a clinic in Paris that would take her,' my father had continued. 'But she wouldn't have anything to do with it. She insisted on the birth. And it killed her of course.'

'I killed her,' I had said.

'It took fourteen years, Nilus. But it got her in the end. A warmer climate might have helped. I tried. God knows, I tried to tempt her away. Every winter I went through the lists. Tangier, Rio, Nairobi. Anywhere at all. It might have saved her. But your mother wouldn't hear of it. But don't blame yourself, don't blame yourself, don't blame yourself, don't blame yourself, don't blame yourself . . .'

'What's that banging?' said Joe.

'What banging?'

'It's coming from upstairs. Like someone's banging on a door.'

'It's just my father.'

'You sure he's all right?'

'Of course he's all right.'

'Sounds like he needs help.'

'It's only catharsis,' I said. 'It's how he works out his temper.'

'Temper?'

'Yes, temper. Passion, petulance.'

'Okay, Nilus. Keep your hair on. Only asked. Catharsis, you say?'

'Catharsis. He bangs about.'

'Don't you think you'd maybe better check?'

'He doesn't like people disturbing him. Not when he's at his catharsis. You want some more tea, cha, brew?'

'Why d'you keep repeating yourself?'

'You want some tea or not?'

'Yeah, why not. Does he do that often?'

'Look, I don't want to talk about it. All right, okay, that fair?'

'Yeah. All right, Nilus. That's fair. Okay. Don't lose your hair. Look, I'm not staying long. I just wanted to know if you had any news of Ira.'

'What about Ira?'

'I thought she might come here. That's all. I just thought . . .'

I exploded. 'Why the fuck should Ira come here? She doesn't even know I'm alive! She doesn't even know I'm living, breathing, sentient!'

'Ira?'

I was shouting, I knew. But in reality, my shouting was on some sort of automatic pilot. Deep down, I was thinking, poor Ira. She doesn't know what she's let herself in for. My mother was the same. She'd been old for a first baby.

Just like Ira – so fragile, delicate like a high-heeled shoe – was far too young. Everything was so unfortunate, brain-chilled, disturbed. It was such a shame.

'God, Nilus. I really love that girl. Though, by rights, I should hate her. I mean her family. God knows, I've got reason. Getting the pigs to lock me up like that. Her Da. But I don't know. Maybe it takes a week in the clink to get your thinking straight. Work out who you are. I mean, from my cell I could hear the birds singing in the dawn, and then the sun would rise, I'd see it maybe for half an hour through a squint in the side window, then it'd pass away overhead, and that was it. I don't know, Nilus, I never thought about birdsong before. And you get to think about flowers, and weeding, and you think, if Ira and me had ourselves a little house now, it would be time to mow the lawn, or weed the flowers, you know, just ordinary things. You with me?'

'You'd look pretty silly weeding flowers this time of the year,' I said.

'Why's that?'

'Whoever heard of anyone weeding flowers in the middle of the winter?'

'Nilus – it's not winter.'

'Of course it's winter.'

'Nilus – it's August. It's the end of the summer. We're in the middle of a heat wave here, Nilus. Are you having me on?'

'Yes,' I said, quickly. 'I'm having you on. Of course I'm having you on.'

'What's up with you, Nilus?'

'There's nothing up with me.'

'Are you all right?'

'I'm fine.'

'And what's that banging upstairs?'

'What banging?'

'Upstairs, Nilus.'

'I told you already. It's my father.'

'That's not your father. That's not coming from your father's room.'

'Is it not?'

'Who's up there, Nilus? I want to know.'

'You want to know, fathom, apprehend?'

'Why d'you keep doing that?'

'Doing what?'

'Keep rehashing the words you use.'

'I don't know. I have to make sure. Sure that people understand me. You can't trust words. You can't trust anything any more. There's brainchill everywhere.'

Except I hadn't said any of that. All I'd said was, 'I don't know.'

'There's someone shouting now. I can hear them.'

Something had to be done. I had to pull myself together. I sighed. 'Oh dear,' I said. 'I was trying to keep it as a surprise. But I should've known you'd find out before – Well anyway. You want to come up and see? Remember, it was supposed to be a surprise.'

'All right. Let's go.'

In the hall, I hesitated a moment. The banging had suddenly stopped. 'The thing is, we'd better check the basement first.'

'Why the basement? The banging was upstairs.'

'It's stopped.'

'But there's someone shouting now. Screaming. Help, is it? Sounds like a woman. Who've you got up there?'

'Don't be silly, Joe. That's a record I left playing.'

'A record?'

'Look Joe. Have you never had anyone give you a surprise before? Don't you know you're not supposed to ask questions?'

He still looked doubtful. 'Where's the door to the basement, then?'

I led him through the kitchen to the larder. 'There.'

'Well?'

'Well, open it, of course.'

He opened the door. 'Now what?'

I was really getting exasperated with all his shilly-shallying. 'Look Joe, just go down the steps a bit. For God's sake, Joe. What d'you think I'm going to do? Lock you in and throw away the key? For God's sake.'

He felt his way down one or two steps.

I slammed the door closed, locked it, and tossed away the key.

Mrs Houlihan was there behind me. 'Okey-dokey, another mouth to feed. And we're nearly out of broth as it is.'

'We'll sort something out,' I said.

I knocked on Ira's door, on my way back to my father's bedroom. 'You're all right, Ira,' I called. 'I didn't let on. We're safe a while yet.'

Her hammering on the door had ceased completely now, Instead there were only moans and groans coming from inside.

'Ira's in her confinement,' I told my father informatively. 'Mrs Houlihan said something about contractions. Not to worry, Mrs Houlihan seems to know what she's talking about.'

My father laughed.

'Are you not worried about Ira?'

'Nilus, my boy, I spend sleepless days and wakeless nights worrying about her.'

I laughed now. My father was in such a good mood. I decided to do him a favour. I lifted up a corner of his mattress, checked underneath. 'Your sheet-folds are in shocking order,' I said. I had to push him over on to his back, to rectify them. He toppled over, limberly. But I soon had the sheets folded perfectly.

I settled my father back in his proper disposition: face slanting upwards, the corners of his eyes on the electric chandelier, his body crooked and sideways.

Surprisingly, he'd lost his rigidity over the months. The flesh had withered to the appearance and texture of parchment. The brandy hadn't been a total success. When I studied them next to his, my own hands, white as blank paper, looked oddly death-like in comparison. The bones from which his flesh was hanging, looked so frail, dainty, with their muscles perishing away, it was a wonder they'd ever managed to support his frame. The smell was vile.

'Thanks, Nilus,' he said. 'You're such a comfort to me.'

'Am I?' It was pleasant to know I could be a comfort to my father. 'Dad? About my birth.'

'What now?'

'I'm not annoyed, Dad. Not now. I'd just like – I don't know – to hear it again.'

'Go on, then, Nilus. Ask me.'

I was quite enjoying this. I felt we were finally getting down to a father and son conversation. A 'talk' at last: but this time, a good old heart to heart, conducted man to man. Even the sight of him and the smell of him and all the rotting breakfasts and suppers littering the room, all untouched, with a celeste putrescence of soft downy mould formed on top, even his face cracked to its eternal ironic grin: nothing really bothered me. I was just happy to be talking with my father. Our differences were resolved.

161

'Tell me again why you wanted my mother to murder me,' I asked. Then I burst out giggling, as though it was the stupidest, most childish request imaginable. I mean, as if all you had to do was look at me and you'd understand immediately why.

He seemed to chuckle a bit too. I liked this. We were sharing a private joke. Father and son, laughing together.

I persisted, still giggling. 'Why did you beg, crave, solicit her, I mean actually beg, crave, solicit her, to have an abortion? In the letters, I mean. Why, Dad? I just want to hear the reason again.' I shrugged a little, embarrassed by my precocity, at the same time approaching a cachinnation as uproarious as Mrs Houlihan's.

'Nilus,' he said, 'there's one thing I want you to know. I want you never to forget this as long as ever you might live. The clinic I had in mind for your mother and yourself, it offered the best abortions either money or solicitation could procure, secure or come by.'

Another time I might have considered he was mocking me, aping my triplications like that. Today I knew he was only trying to help. He was on my side. Our side.

'Thanks, Dad,' I said, simpering through a sort of cosy candescence of gratitude and affection.

'Don't mention it,' he said. 'A pleasure.'

'We'll have to do something about Ira,' I said. 'I mean, about her baby. We don't want anything to happen. Not to Ira. I think I kind of like her, you see. She's maybe not completely orderly. But she's learning. She's already stopped hammering on her door. I think I like her.'

'Poor lamb, of course you do,' said Mrs Houlihan. I didn't know where she'd come from. She'd just appeared out of nowhere, the way she did.

'I mean, I don't want her to die, giving birth. Birth's such a haphazard affair.'

'What you mean is: birth could be the death of her,' said my father, jocularly.

We all laughed.

'Look what it did to your mother,' sighed Mrs Houlihan, after the hilarity.

'And what's the point anyway?' I asked.

'Sure they just come and take away your home afterwards.'

'Exactly,' I said.

'What's the point?' asked Mrs Houlihan.

I had no answer. I had no answer at all.

When I'd fetched John Mitchell and Father Mulcahy and sat them down in their correct places in my father's bedroom, I went to collect Ira. I opened the door. She was lying face upwards on top of her bed. She had her legs and arms stiffly splayed, supporting the balloon in the middle of her night-dress. She looked silly. If she'd just let her bottom rest on the bed, she wouldn't have had to look like a crab, or a lobster, one of those creeping things. She could have lain normally. She was groaning away, tossing the blankets, every now and then emitting a God-awful shriek.

God knows what state her sheets are in, I thought. Then I felt mean, thinking that. The poor girl was in pain. In terrible pain, anger, anguish, by all accounts. I had to help her.

When I tried to lift her, it was like struggling with a lion, or tiger, or puma, or cougar, or an injured jaguar. One of those running things.

'Hell hath no fury,' remarked Mrs Houlihan, who'd crept up behind me again, 'like a woman in her confinement.'

'Mrs Houlihan,' I said, 'perhaps we could have less of your platitudes and more of your assistance.'

Together we managed to drag her, lift her, drop her, pick her up, jostle and wrest her into my father's bedroom. She collapsed in an exhausted heap on my father's bed, still shrieking, and groaning, and jerking her body up and down, east and west.

It was a terrible messy business. I wondered had her balloon sprung a leak. I'd have to go back and clean the carpet later.

The banging from the basement downstairs was getting louder and more tempersome. By the second. Or the aeon. I couldn't distinguish those periods any more.

'Right,' I said, 'we're all here.'

Mrs Houlihan smiled her lingering smile, my father grinned his crooked grin, Father Mulcahy darted warily his eyes, John Mitchell gazed above and to the right in his usual puzzled surprise.

'Tell me a story, Dad.'

'A story of what?'

'Like you used to. About the old things. *Fadó, fadó.* About the hedge priests and the blind bards and the old ridden hag who comes to young Irish poets in their dreams, begging for Spanish wine and, in the twinkling of her eyes, she discards her cloak and she's a beautiful young lady before you.'

I'd got all that out without a single triplication. I was quite pleased, happy, content with myself.

'Mrs Houlihan's here now. And the hedge priest. And the blind bard. You've gathered them all to you, Nilus. Isn't that story enough for you?'

'No,' I said, simply. Because it wasn't enough. It was just never enough.

'Then ask Mrs Houlihan. She'll tell you her own story.'

'Poor lamb,' said Mrs Houlihan. 'Sure, I've no stories

left. I'm done for, in the story department. Them poets have me all beached up. But your father will tell you, isn't that so? Poor Nilus.' And she discarded her frayed and faded cloak, and I saw that all along she'd been a beautiful young woman in disguise. She didn't look exactly like my mother, not exactly as I remembered her. But I knew who she was. She was the beautiful mother I'd never known but had only been able to worship in the framed photographs by my matt black jigsaw, taken in her nurse's uniform before I was born and she was forced to give up nursing. 'Poor Nilus,' she said, in her young and beautiful voice.

Ira let out a shuddering shriek. And was silent. She seemed to have fallen into a wretched sleep on the bed. Or a coma, maybe. In the dark and the dread of her labour.

The banging from downstairs was torrential in my brain.

'Well, Nilus,' said my father, and immediately there was a summer's evening. An evening when my father did tell me a story and when perhaps my mother didn't die, and the perfume works hadn't moved its entrance, or the cottages been bulldozed, and barges were on the canal, or maybe the opposite, I wasn't sure: just an evening when I heard my father's soft and antique voice. 'Well Nilus,' he said, 'it was a sort of meantime. And in that meantime, few as we were, we waited, though it didn't exactly feel like waiting, if you catch my meaning, for we were still very busy engaged in eking out some manner of an existence, and yet I suppose we were waiting at the bottom of it. And as the bread was baking and the broth on the boil, and the building men constructed with the noise and rattle of their motorized trucks, I suppose at the same time we were waiting, our eyes were vigilant, we were ready. And as the leaves fell in their showers so that old men were employed to collect them in bincarts, for it was the autumn that was coming, and nearly gone at that, we waited less patiently, believing it wouldn't be too long now. And it was all very grand the way we did things then, for we'd put away in darkened cupboards the most of our scruples and we seemed to be working together and pulling away together and the many varied hands pulling and all together and the hands of the women pulling with us and the children laughing excitedly and urging us on in the streets as we passed and we passed with our shoulders flung against our shadows, marching to the music of our feet, which sounded like the thunder of the movement of man, and it was all very grand.'

The banging was on my father's bedroom door now. Cracks were splintering in the mouldings. It was interesting to note which mouldings gave way first. Such a disturbance. Over the banging and the thin strains of 'Nobody's Child' that I fumbled on my mother's piano accordion, somewhere inside or outside my brain, and the chill on my brain, I heard a baby's tiny disturbed voice – so tiny a listening ear might crush it . . . crying.